by
Helen Fine

Illustrated by
Hal Just

UNION OF AMERICAN
HEBREW CONGREGATIONS
New York

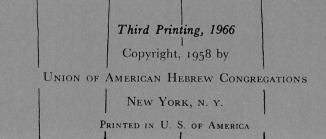

Third Printing, 1966

Copyright, 1958 by

UNION OF AMERICAN HEBREW CONGREGATIONS

NEW YORK, N. Y.

PRINTED IN U. S. OF AMERICA

EDITOR'S
INTRODUCTION

G'DEE IS ANOTHER "FIRST" IN THE LONG SERIES OF
unique books for Jewish education published by the Union of
American Hebrew Congregations. Helen Fine sought to tell the
story of some of the Jewish holidays but, looking for a technique
of bringing a new and fresh approach to the subject, she hit on
the idea of having an American Jewish child receive as a gift from
Israel a little kid. Through the eyes of this little goat we see the
entire Jewish year, beginning with the Sabbath and going through
with a little amusing mischief the various Jewish holidays throughout the year. The author sought to emphasize the religious values
inherent in each of the holidays, not merely by describing the signif-
icance of each day but also by seeking to associate the essence of
the holiday with the story of G'dee.

For example, we may consider the Yom Kippur story, "Please
Forgive G'dee." The "poor kid" chews up the panda, eats the
blackberry pie, chews the knobs off the television set as well as a
tire on one of the cars, but the children ask God to forgive G'dee
for all the wrongs he had done.

> Dear God, please forgive,
> Forgive us this day.
> And keep us from harm,
> We earnestly pray.

The naughtiness of G'dee is charmingly described but the writing,
while interesting in itself, manages to stress throughout the love of
children for a helpless little kid. Thus, the idea of צער בעלי חיים
—compassion for living creatures—which is one of the great religious values of the Jewish tradition is emphasized throughout.

While this booklet may be used as a text for children in the
lower grades, it will no doubt find its way into the hands of many
a child for pleasure reading. Not enough books of this type have
been written for Jewish children and we have every confidence that
Helen Fine will be encouraged to write more to the delight of Jewish
children.

EMANUEL GAMORAN

ACKNOWLEDGMENTS

IT ALL BEGAN IN THE RELIGIOUS SCHOOL CLASS
when the children asked for a story. A little white goat scampered
out of imagination and wandered into the hearts of the children.
They clamored for more—and more—and more—.

The children inspired and the grown-ups helped to bring the
dream to fulfilment.

Especially:

My beloved rabbi, Roland B. Gittelsohn, G'dee's godfather,
whose faith and friendship are a constant source of encouragement
and inspiration.

Rabbi Eugene B. Borowitz, whose friendly advice and deep
understanding has never wavered during the innumerable hours he
has spent in preparing this book for publication.

Mrs. Barnett R. Brickner and the late Dr. Brickner, of blessed
memory, whose vision prodded me to write a book using experiences
in the teaching field.

The Reading Committee of the Commission on Jewish Education, Rabbis Leon Fram, Harry J. Stern, and James A. Wax, whose
invaluable criticisms and suggestions have improved the book im-
measurably.

Mr. Samuel Nemzoff, who has always given kindly assistance
in the endless research for source materials.

Mr. Hal Just, whose whimsical illustrations help delightfully
to translate the text.

Mr. Ralph Davis, whose devotion has produced a skilfully-
designed book from beginning to end, and Miss Sylvia Schiff, whose
error-catching eyes have kept G'dee from tripping over his punc-
tuation.

Macmillan Publishing Co. for permission to quote from *Barter*
by Sara Teasdale.

My grateful thanks to all of you.

HELEN FINE

Contents

A Crown Prince for the Sabbath

THE GREEN TRUCK CAME TO A grinding halt in front of the white ranch house. The driver jumped out and opened the rear door. With a quick tug he lifted a heavy wooden crate with a small hole on the top onto his shoulders. Up a flagstone walk he trudged. Depositing the crate he pressed the bell under a sign that said, MANN.

Mrs. Mann came to the door, followed by her eight-year-old twins, Debra and David.

"I have a crate for Debra and David Mann, all the way from the State of Israel," announced the driver.

"It's Uncle Joseph's surprise," shouted David.

"Ma-a-a-a," came a strange voice from inside. David and Debra peered into the hole.

"It's a goat!" yelled David.

"It's a goat!" echoed Debra.

"No!" cried Mrs. Mann in astonishment.

"Sign here!" said the driver with a big grin.

Mrs. Mann signed the card and the driver ran down the walk chuckling, "Good luck to you, Mrs. Mann."

Quickly Mother and the twins pried open the crate with a hammer. Out jumped a small white goat. Tied around its neck was a white envelope addressed to David and Debra Mann. Mrs. Mann removed the letter, and read it, the twins peering over her shoulder.

> *Dear Debra and David:*
> I promised to send you a special surprise for your eighth birthday, and here it is. His name is G'dee which is the Hebrew word for goat. G'dee is a very smart goat, and I hope he will bring you much happiness.
> With love,
> UNCLE JOSEPH

The twins' blue eyes danced.

"A little white goat all our own!" said Debra, hugging G'dee on the left side.

"This is a lucky Friday for the Manns," said David, hugging G'dee on the right side.

A frown creased Mrs. Mann's forehead. "What will Daddy say?" she asked, trying to smile a welcome to G'dee.

G'dee gazed at the twins, his heart pounding like a trip hammer. He lifted his pointed head and looked all about him. He ma-a-a-a-ed once and then again. "I'm going to love my new home," he bleated, "and best of all I'm going to love these jolly twins." With a sigh of contentment he lay down on the carpet. His eyelids slipped down over his eyes, and G'dee was instantly asleep, one paw tucked under his beard.

"Poor tired little goat," said Debra.

"Traveling all the way from the State of Israel is no hop, skip, and a jump," said David.

One by one David and Debra and Mrs. Mann tiptoed into the kitchen and shut the door. They talked quietly so as not to disturb their sleeping visitor.

Debra looked at the worried frown on Mother's face. "Mother, Daddy won't mind. You'll see."

David said, "Daddy said that we could have a dog for our birthday. So what difference does it make if it's a goat, instead?"

The door key sounded in the latch of the front door. A startled voice said, "What in the world is this? Why, it's a goat as I live and breathe!"

The twins opened the kitchen door and saw Daddy staring at G'dee. His eyes were twin question marks. They

4

stared G'dee awake from his deep sleep. G'dee examined Daddy for a second and bounded over to David, nuzzling into his legs. David held him firmly by the right horn. Debra came over to hold him just as firmly by the left horn.

Daddy stood there saying nothing.

Mother broke the silence. "Your brother, Joe, sent him from Israel for the twins' birthday. His name is G'dee which is the Hebrew word for goat." Mother gave Daddy the information with a twinkle in her eyes.

"If this is Joe's idea of a joke, I don't like his sense of humor," said Daddy, frowning at his family.

G'dee slipped out of the twins' grasp and ran over to snuggle into Daddy's legs. Daddy touched G'dee's soft silky coat. The frown melted away and a smile appeared.

"All right, twins, I'm listening," said Daddy, stroking G'dee's fur.

"Look, Dad, Debra and I would much rather have a goat than a dog," said David, turning to Debra for encouragement.

"Please say yes, Daddy, please?" Debra dimpled up at Dad with shining eyes.

Mr. Mann turned to Mrs. Mann. "What do *you* say, dear? Goats have a bad reputation for mischief, you know. G'dee may be *Mr. Mischief* himself."

G'dee scrambled over to Mother and looked up at her. "Who me?" he bleated cockily at her, "Mr. Mischief! Indeed! He's talking about another goat on another planet." Mother laughed right out loud, and at that very instant G'dee became a treasured member of the Mann family.

When the sun set, the family gathered around the piano in the living-room. G'dee saw David and Debra put two white candles into two carved silver candlesticks.

"May the Sabbath Light bring peace to our hearts, and shed blessings of peace on our happy home," said Mrs. Mann.

5

She struck a match and lit the two wicks. G'dee watched the candles leap into twin flames casting a rosy glow on the smiling faces belonging to his new family.

"Boruch ato Adonoi Elohenu melech ho-olom asher kidshonu b'mitzvosov v'tzivonu l'hadlik ner shel Shabos," said Mrs. Mann.

"Blessed art Thou, O Lord, our God, Ruler of the world, who has blessed us by His commandments, and commanded us to light the Sabbath candles," chanted the twins, looking down at their new goat. Debra bent down toward G'dee. "This is the way our family welcomes the Sabbath, G'dee. You see, Daddy is an engineer and he worked hard at the office all week. Mother worked hard at home. David and I worked hard in school. Shabos means rest. When we stop our work we can think about right and wrong, and whether we're doing right. That's why the Sabbath makes us feel close to God. That's why it's a holy day."

G'dee licked Debra's left cheek with his long pink tongue.

David kneeled down to pat G'dee. "On the Sabbath, Daddy feels like a king. Mother is a queen, Debra is a princess, and I am a prince."

"And what is G'dee? He's part of our family now," laughed Debra.

"Oh, that's easy." David flashed his answer almost without thinking. "G'dee is a crown prince."

G'dee wagged his head up and down in agreement. He liked the new title. "Right you are!" he bleated, licking David's cheek.

When the family sat down to the Sabbath dinner, G'dee looked hungrily at the twisted loaf of bread at the end of the table. He saw the tall silver goblet standing on a brass tray beside a bottle of wine. At each place was a piece of food that he had never seen before and a small silver cup. He

edged over closer to the table to get a good sniff, but stopped in his tracks. His curiosity would have to wait. Things were happening and he didn't want to miss any of them, no, not one single thing.

G'dee saw Debra walk over to Mrs. Mann's chair. She stood quietly and bowed her head. Mother placed her hand over Debra's head and said softly, "Be thou blessed, my darling daughter, as Sara, Rebecca, Rachel, and Leah. Be the pride of thy parents, and a blessing to Israel and to all mankind."

Debra sat down. G'dee saw David rise and walk over to Mr. Mann's chair. He, too, stood quietly and bowed his head. Daddy placed his hand over David's head. "Blessed be thou, my dear son, as Ephraim and Menassah. Be the pride of thy parents, and a blessing to all of Israel," said Mr. Mann. David returned to his seat.

David and Debra whispered together, looking at G'dee.

"Daddy," said David, "Debra and I have decided to bless G'dee. He's our new child."

"Why not?" said Daddy, winking at Mother.

David placed his hand on G'dee's right horn, and Debra placed her hand on G'dee's left horn.

"Be thou blessed, our little white goat," said David.

"Be the pride of all our family," said Debra.

G'dee cuddled into the twins. "I'll try mighty hard," he bleated, cocking his head to the side, and running back to the head of the table. That food was still waiting for him. But, no! Things were still happening.

G'dee watched Daddy pour some red wine into his silver goblet. Mother poured some into the other goblets. Holding out the cup before him, Daddy said, "Boruch ato Adonoi Elohenu melech ho-olom bore p'ri ha-gofen." The twins said together, "Blessed art Thou, O Lord, our God, Ruler of the world, who creates the fruit of the vine." Daddy took

8

a sip of wine. Mother took a sip of wine. Debra took a sip of wine and David took a sip of wine.

"Now," bleated G'dee, "it should be my turn," and sure enough it was! David bent down with his goblet. "Here G'dee, take a sip from my Kiddush cup."

G'dee dipped his tongue into the sweet wine. Everyone laughed when G'dee lapped it up to the very last drop. "Very good," he bleated, licking a drop of wine that had wandered down into his beard.

"Now for the food on that plate!" ma-a-a-ed G'dee, smacking his lips hungrily, and edging over to the table again. But no! Not yet!

G'dee saw Daddy cut a slice of the chalo on the table. "Boruch ato Adonoi Elohenu melech ho-olom, hamotzi lechem min ho-oretz." Daddy broke the chalo into small pieces and put them on a plate.

"Blessed art Thou, O Lord, our God, Ruler of the world, who brings forth bread from the earth," said the twins.

Daddy ate a piece and passed the bread to Mother. Mother ate a piece and passed the plate to David. David ate a piece and passed the bread to Debra. G'dee looked hungrily at Debra. "My turn now, Debra," he bleated, leaping up at Debra, almost knocking the plate out of her hand. She put the plate on the carpet for G'dee.

"M-m-m-m-m, delicious," bleated G'dee, gobbling up the bread.

9

And now came the Sabbath meal. Meal! It was a Feast! G'dee discovered that the food on the plate that he had been watching was chopped liver. G'dee ate his in one gulp. He lapped up the chicken soup with noodles floating in its golden goodness. He smacked his lips over the roast chicken and the fluffy lemon pie.

"Crown Prince, you are a lucky goat," he bleated. "Your new mother cooks like a queen, a true Sabbath queen."

After dinner G'dee joined the family singing the Sabbath songs. G'dee liked "Sholom Aleichem" best of all the joyous z'miros.

Right in the middle of the last song G'dee fell fast asleep. He was so tired. "After all," he thought, "Debra said that the Sabbath was a day of rest, and I am just the goat who deserves a good long rest."

Debra said, "I've written a new poem about the Sabbath, and I simply can't think of a good last line."

"Let's hear it," said Daddy, "maybe we can help."

Debra stood up and looked lovingly at her family.

The Sun goes down
Each Friday night.
And Sabbath's here
With its delight.

The Sabbath table's
Gaily spread
At Daddy's place
Are wine and bread.

We light the candles,
Chant a prayer,
The music's sweet
Beyond compare.

Daddy says Kiddush,
Then gives us some wine,
Sipping its goodness
Together is fine.

Over the Chalo
A blessing is said,
My how I love it,
My favorite bread.

Sabbath each week
Is a family treat,

Debra stopped. "And this is where I'm stuck," she said, looking hopefully at her family.

Daddy was ready in a flash.

Sabbath each week
Is a family treat,
Now we've G'dee
To make it complete.

G'dee squinted one eye open, and rolled over. "Spoken in the true Sabbath spirit," he bleated, dropping off to sleep again.

Mr. Mischief,
Indeed!

G'DEE GREW TO LOVE HIS NEW FAM-
ily more and more each day. The breezeway joining the
garage to the house was his bedroom. The twins' plastic
swimming pool filled with straw was G'dee's bed. Mr. Mann
had to store extra straw in the garage because G'dee insisted
on eating his bed every night.

In the morning when the twins awoke, they ran to the
breezeway. G'dee greeted them with a loud bleat, stamping
his legs impatiently. "It's about time," he ma-a-a-ed, "it's
no fun cooped up in here. All outdoors is waiting for me!"
Leaping up on David, he crowded him to the door.

"Take it easy, G'dee. Give me a chance to get the key
into the door," laughed David.

"Hurry, hurry, hurry! Those plump juicy grasshoppers
have been fiddling their wings at me since dawn," G'dee
bleated, giving David another shove.

David flung open the door. G'dee was a swift arrow as
he shot out. Once outside G'dee scooted around the house,
lickety split, as if a thousand wolves were chasing him. Once
around and twice around, and once around again—and then

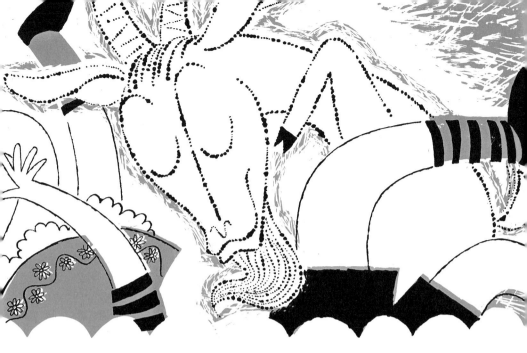

—without any warning, G'dee dove into the twins, tumbling them to the ground.

Tangle—wangle—jangle—legs waved frantically in the air—Debra legs—David legs—G'dee legs—all jumbled together like a jigsaw puzzle. Debra's screams and David's shrieks and G'dee's squeals ripped the air.

Mother ran out alarmed. "Enough of this wild playing," she scolded, "someone's bound to get hurt in this free-for-all." She untangled the tangle and held G'dee's horn.

G'dee panted up at her with shining eyes. "Now don't you fret, lovely lady," he bleated. "I'm always carerful to keep my horns in a safe place. I wouldn't hurt the twins. I love them too much."

When school began the twins went each day to the third grade in the Lawrence School. G'dee trotted along between them. Near the school door he did a smart about-face and scrambled down the stairs wagging his snub-nosed tail. "So long, twins," he ma-a-a-ed to the door, "I'd rather be an ignorant goat if you don't mind."

Back to the garden G'dee ran. He had interesting things to do while waiting for the twins—very interesting things.

Daddy's velvety lawn needed his attention. G'dee pawed the grass, and ran his nose along the ground looking for grasshoppers. *Pounce!* A fat grasshopper hopped into his mouth. And another—and another—and another—it took ten to satisfy G'dee's grasshopper appetite.

He looked behind him. Down the smooth lawn marched a straight line of dug-up heaps of dirt. *Good!* Now he could play *leap goat*. Over the mounds he sailed like a stunt airplane, his beard waving in the wind—up and down—up and down—

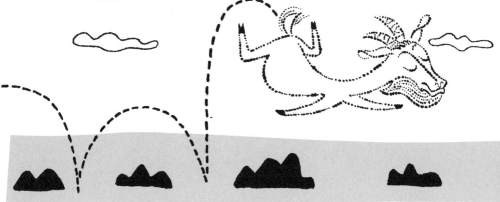

Now for something different! G'dee spied a brown snake. *Pounce!* No luck this time! The snake wrinkled across the grass and was gone. "Oh, well," bleated the goat, "you can't have everything."

He wandered over to some tall hollyhocks leaning their heads against the garden wall. A humming-bird helicoptered above the bright flowers, its emerald green breast glittering in the sun. G'dee jumped high in the air. A whir of fluttering wings rushed past G'dee's nose as he crash-landed in the middle of the hollyhocks, crushing them with his sudden weight.

"Ouch!" bleated G'dee, making a sour face at the humming-bird, now a jeweled speck in the blue sky.

He moved across the lawn to Daddy's prize tulip bulbs. "I'd better stick to things that don't move," he ma-a-a-ed. Deep down into the spongy earth he dug. "Why, they taste almost like onions," he thought, as he munched away. Two round goat tears trickled out of the corners of his eyes. Mrs. Mann cried when *she* peeled onions, and he would, too.

After the bulb feast, G'dee spied Tiger, the next-door cat, dozing in the sun on the fence. Scrambling over, he bleated loudly, scaring Tiger off the fence. G'dee chased the cat through a small opening under the porch. Tiger's round green eyes laughed at him from the safe place.

G'dee heard Mrs. Mann back the car out of the garage. He dashed over to the car. Mrs. Mann waved to him. "Mind the house, G'dee. I'll be back in an hour."

G'dee felt proud to be trusted with the care of the house. Into the house he sauntered to keep a close watch. He found work there that kept him busy. Debra's panda had to be chewed, and the sawdust scattered all over the bedroom floor. The freshly baked blueberry pie cooling on the kitchen table had to be eaten. The knobs on the television set had to be tasted. To his disgust, G'dee discovered that the knobs left splinters on his tongue.

He spied a box of soap flakes on the kitchen sink, and knocked it off with his horn. Kicking the box in front of him, he spread a flaky path through the kitchen and the living-room. "The broadloom rug looks pretty with that white streak running through it," he bleated, proudly.

He wandered outside again. He noticed some white sheets on the clothes-line flapping in the breeze. "I bet I can pull those sheets off," he bragged to himself. G'dee was right. He could and he did. He found himself rolled up in one of the sheets like a mummy. His feet helped him to kick his way out leaving the white sheet dirty with the marks of goat feet. Of course the sheet was torn in a dozen places.

G'dee rolled over on the grass. Pulling the clothes off the line was hard work. He decided to take a short nap. A huge orange and black monarch butterfly cruising along perched on G'dee's right horn to rest its tired wings. But G'dee slept on and on under the smiling sun.

A clanging bell pierced the stillness. G'dee was awake in an instant. "The school bell," he thought, "the twins are out of school at last!" He sprinted across the lawn and down the street toward the school. David and Debra were coming down the steps just as he arrived. With a joyous ma-a-a-a, he sprang at them, hugging them with his front paws. "Oh, how I've missed you all day," he bleated. "Nothing can compare to the fun we have together."

When they came home Mother was waiting for them. The look in her eyes told them plainly that all was not peaceful in the Mann household. Mother didn't say anything. She took each of her children by the hand and led them on a grand inspection tour around the house.

They saw Panda's sawdust on the floor of Debra's bedroom.

They examined the splintery knobs of the television set.

They followed the streak of soap flakes throughout the house.

G'dee took the guided tour, too. He wondered why nobody was talking. He had never seen the twins and Mother so quiet since he had come to Brookline. An idea began to hatch in his goat brain. Could his family be angry at him? No, that couldn't be possible! "I worked much too hard," he bleated. "They just can't get over what I was able to do in so short a time."

The grand tour continued, this time outside the house.

They saw what remained of Daddy's prize tulip bulbs.

They followed the dug-up mounds on the velvety grass, and they saw the crushed hollyhocks.

Last of all they saw the holes made by sharp goat feet in the sheets scattered about under the clothes-line in the backyard.

Mother spoke at last. "Well, twins, what are we going to do? G'dee simply can't keep up this kind of mischief."

"He certainly can't," agreed David and Debra at the same time.

G'dee cocked his head. "Oh, dear! They really are cross with me!" He backed away from the sad faces in front of him, bleating sorrowfully.

"Mother, when David and I were babies we managed to get into plenty of mischief because we didn't know any better. But you and Daddy taught us to behave. David and I will simply have to teach G'dee how to be good too." Debra bent down to G'dee. "Please try, G'dee. Please try to be a good goat."

David shook his head at Debra. "That isn't going to get you anywhere at all, Debra. I think I know a better way to impress G'dee. Watch!"

David took G'dee's horn. He guided him back to all the places where he had done his mischief. Debra and Mother followed, wondering what David was planning to do.

At each place David looked G'dee squarely in the eyes. His voice was firm as he shook his finger at G'dee. "Never again! You must never, never, never do this damage again!"

G'dee *was* impressed. He bobbed his head to the right and he bobbed his head to the left. He promised with his eyes to try very hard to behave himself. "Do you think for one minute that I want to be a naughty goat?" he bleated. "I'm much too happy here in my new home. I love you with all my heart. I was just trying to make the time pass quickly until you returned from school."

G'dee soon learned to be good in the middle of the week when the twins were at school, but he still didn't like being lonely.

Best of all, yes, best of all, was Sunday, for Sunday the twins went to religious school with G'dee tagging along. G'dee enjoyed going to religious school with the twins. The Manns lived very close to the Temple Israel Religious School on the Riverway in Boston, just over the Brookline town line.

In back of the school was a garden bordered by high bushes. The garden was a perfect place for a goat to wait until school was over. Here G'dee could frisk about, kicking up his feet and chasing his tail. When the bells for recess rang the children called to G'dee from the open windows.

"Here, G'dee," called Stephen from the open window. He tossed down a bag of pop-corn. It hit G'dee square on the horn. Poppity pop! The pop-corn went down G'dee's throat smoothly.

"Here, G'dee," called Susan. She flung out a bag of potato chips. It hit G'dee square on the tail. Crunchity crunch! The potato chips crackled down G'dee's throat.

"Here, G'dee," called Jeffery. He threw down a whipped cream puff. The puff splashed white against G'dee's beard. Lappity-lap! G'dee's long tongue lipped up and down and across his frosted beard.

18

The children weren't the only ones to shower G'dee with gifts. Mr. Samuel, the principal, had his own special welcome for G'dee too. At eleven o'clock every Sunday morning, Mr. Samuel appeared in the garden. As soon as G'dee spied him he streaked across the grass and nosed about in Mr. Samuel's coat pocket. G'dee was never disappointed. Into the pocket would go a hand and out would come three squares of sugar. Into G'dee's mouth popped the first piece —and the second piece—and the third piece.

"Thank you, kindly, Mr. Principal," bleated G'dee, wagging a joyful tail, "religious school is a delicious place to visit."

A Happy New Year

IT WAS THE DAY BEFORE ROSH HA-shono. The twins were busy in the playroom downstairs addressing New Year cards to their friends. David was printing the addresses, and Debra was pasting the stamps on the envelopes. G'dee was helping, too. He licked the back of the stamps with his long tongue. "Glue on the back of stamps is very tasty," he bleated, "that is, if you're a goat."

"I bet G'dee would like to say Happy New Year to everyone this year too," said David suddenly.

"It's too bad goats can't talk. Tomorrow when we go to the Children's Service at Temple Israel everyone will say 'Happy New Year' to G'dee, and G'dee won't be able to answer," said Debra. She heaved a sigh. At the same time her brain exploded with an idea.

"David! I've an idea! Why can't we tie a sign on G'dee's horn? We could make it out of cardboard and print HAPPY NEW YEAR on it."

No sooner said than done. Debra cut out an oblong cardboard, and David printed HAPPY NEW YEAR on it with heavy black ink. Debra punched a hole in the cardboard and pulled

20

a string through it. G'dee watched curiously. David attached the sign to G'dee's horn, tying it with a secure knot.

The sign stood up proudly for everyone to see. G'dee stretched tall as he paraded around the playroom. "Thank you, twins," he bleated, "I'm glad you thought of such a clever idea. I'd like to say Happy New Year on Rosh Hashono, too."

Mother and Daddy came downstairs. Mother was carrying a large bowl of peeled apples, and a small pitcher of honey.

Daddy looked at G'dee's sign. "That is some sign," he said with a chuckle, patting G'dee on the back.

Mother looked at the sign. "That is a beautiful sign." She set the apples and honey on the table.

Everyone gathered around the table. Each one took a piece of apple and dipped it into the honey.

"For a sweet year," said Daddy.

"For a sugar sweet year," said Mother.

"For a candy sweet year," said Debra.

"For a honey sweet year," said David.

G'dee bleated impatiently. "What are you waiting for? I'm a member of this family too."

Debra popped a slice of honeyed apple into his open mouth. David did the same thing. Naturally G'dee ate most of the apples and most of the honey. He licked the inside of the pitcher with his long tongue. Round and round the glass went his tongue until not a drop of honey remained.

> Apples and honey,
> Oh, my, what a treat!
> Making our New Year
> So happy and sweet,

sang Debra, dancing around the playroom.

On Rosh Ha-shono morning the Mann family walked to the temple for the special children's services.

> On Rosh Ha-shono every year
> We hear the shofor loud and clear.
> A Happy New Year it calls to you,
> A Happy New Year to every Jew.

Debra chanted her poem as she skipped along. As they walked along Commonwealth Avenue they greeted friends on every side.

"Happy New Year," said Mr. and Mrs. Mann.

"Happy New Year," said David and Debra.

"Happy New Year," said G'dee's sign as he waggled his straggly whiskers.

Everyone smiled. The children crowded about G'dee and patted him on the back.

In front of the temple David tied G'dee to a stone pole. "You'll have to wait outside, G'dee. Animals aren't allowed in the temple."

G'dee cocked his head to the side. "I don't want to be tied up to an old pole," he bleated. "I want to go to the children's services with you." He strained with all his might at the rope and moaned a dismal ma-a-a-a-a.

"Now, G'dee, be a good goat. We'll come for you in a little while," said Debra, giving G'dee a last fond hug.

Up the stairs into the temple walked the Mann family. They sat down on the left side of the aisle, three rows from the back.

The Rosh Ha-shono services began. The twins followed the service in their prayer books. After a while Rabbi Israel **held up** a shofor for the audience to see.

"The shofor is **the** horn of a ram. Our ancestors who lived long ago used the shofor for many reasons. Its blast was heard at the beginning of a new year. When a new king was crowned the shofor was blown. It ushered in the Sabbath, and it proclaimed war. Now, boys and girls, Mr. Isaacs, our cantor, is going to show you how the shofor is used."

Mr. Isaacs put the shofor to his lips and blew a single blast. Its hollow sound rang in the twins' ears. The rabbi said, "This is called the t'kio." Mr. Isaacs raised the shofor to his lips a second time, and this time he blew three broken blasts. "This is called sh'vorim," continued the rabbi. The cantor lifted the shofor once again and blew several short notes, one after another, very quickly. "This is the t'ruo," said the rabbi. "Later in the service you will hear all the shofor sounds joined together."

David whispered to Debra. "That must take a lot of lung power. He must have practiced blowing the shofor for a long time."

"I wish I could try to blow it some time," said Debra.

Mother put her fingers to her lips. The twins listened to the rabbi.

"When we hear the shofor," said the rabbi, "we pray to God to forgive us for all the wrongs that we have done during the year. We pray that we will lead a better life by helping all those about us who need our help. All over the world at this time our Jews are praying. These prayers help us to feel close to each other, wherever we are living."

"Please make me a good girl," prayed Debra with all her heart.

"Please make me a good boy," prayed David with all his heart.

Debra looked at David, and David looked at Debra. "Please make G'dee a good goat," they both prayed, smiling at each other.

They looked up to see Rabbi Israel take the Torah from the holy ark. In honor of Rosh Ha-shono the Torah was dressed in white velvet. The rabbi unrolled the Torah Scroll and pointed to the words with a carved silver pointer.

David and Debra heard the rabbi read the portion of the Torah that is always read on Rosh Ha-shono. After he finished, they read the English translation in their pamphlets. They knew and loved the story of Abraham and how he offered his son, Isaac, to God as a sacrifice.

Rabbi Israel began to speak again. "This story, children,

teaches us a great and wonderful truth. At first, Abraham thought that the best way to prove his love to God was to sacrifice his only son, Isaac. But Abraham was mistaken. Those who believed in idols might want people to sacrifice children but God didn't want Abraham to do this at all. What God wanted was life for Isaac, and life for every other human being in the world. God wanted Abraham to teach Isaac how to live as a good Jew." The rabbi smiled at the upturned faces of the children.

"And now—I have a question to ask. Can anyone tell me another reason why we use the shofor? I'll give you a tiny hint. Think back to the story you have just read."

David almost toppled off his seat waving his hand. The rabbi called on him. David rose and cleared his throat. "In the story Abraham sacrificed a ram instead of Isaac. He found it tangled in some nearby bushes by its horn." David sat down quickly but sprang up again. "Oh, I forgot, our shofor is made from a ram's horn." He sat down, his face red as an apple.

"Very good, David," laughed the rabbi, "I couldn't have explained it better myself."

The services continued. The rabbi told the children a wonderful Rosh Ha-shono story and then it was time for Mr. Isaacs to blow the shofor. Debra, sitting on the end seat, suddenly felt a warm moist nose in her hand. She looked down to see G'dee licking her hand, the broken leash dangling behind him on the carpet.

Before Debra had a chance to do anything about it, the cantor blew the shofor with a mighty blast. "T'kio, sh'vorim, t'ruo," rang the shofor clearly from the pulpit. The twins saw G'dee sprint down the aisle up to the altar steps. He stopped short at the feet of the cantor, and looked up at him curiously.

"T'kio—sh'vorim—t'ruo," sounded the shofor again. This time, G'dee leaped off the altar with a frightened bleat, and bounded down the aisle out the back door. Debra and David ran after him. In the front lobby they saw Mr. Kirkman, the custodian, holding on to G'dee with all his strength, with G'dee straining to get away.

"I caught your religious goat just as he was leaping out the door," chuckled Mr. Kirkman.

"Oh, thank you so much, Mr. Kirkman," cried Debra.

"Forgive G'dee. He's never heard a shofor before. It frightened him, I guess," said David.

"Think nothing of it, children. I'm glad I caught him," said Mr. Kirkman.

"It's a good thing you caught him. G'dee might have had a bad accident running across Commonwealth Avenue," said Debra with thankful eyes.

Please Forgive G'dee

IT WAS YOM KIPPUR EVENING. MR. and Mrs. Mann were at the Kol Nidrei services at the temple. Joseph Adams, who lived across the street, was staying with the twins. Joseph was a freshman at Harvard College, and the twins' favorite baby-sitter. He knew many wonderful magic tricks.

They were sitting in the kitchen. Joseph was showing the twins how to make a cat's face with a piece of string. David and Debra's eyes were riveted on Joseph as they watched him operate the string with great skill.

Suddenly they heard a crash. It came from the living-room.

"G'dee!" shouted the twins.

"G'dee!" shouted Joseph, a startled look on his face.

Before they could investigate, G'dee came bounding into the kitchen, his ears standing up like sentinels. He ran like a bolt of lightning under the kitchen table, hiding his face in his paws. G'dee had good reason to be frightened, as the twins and Joseph soon discovered. In the living-room, on the

28

floor, was Mother's blue and white wedgewood lamp,
broken off at the base.

"Oh!" cried the twins.

"Oh, no!" cried Joseph.

"What will Mother say?" asked Debra.

"What will Father say?" asked David.

Joseph said nothing. He picked up the lamp carefully,
and examined it. Luckily there was a clean break where the
base joined the lamp. "Perhaps someone can mend the
crack so that the break won't show." Joseph was hopeful.

"Do you really think the lamp can be fixed, really and
truly?" asked Debra, a bright tear in her eye.

"I have some money saved up—about $9.00. Do you
think that will be enough? Do you, Joseph, do you?" asked
David.

"Let's wait until your parents come home from the temple," advised Joseph.

Back into the kitchen they trotted. G'dee peeped out from
under the table. He looked up at the twins with sad goat

eyes. No one said a single word—not one single word. Poor G'dee! He was in disgrace. The sad faces in front of him were more than he could bear. No one loved him any more. He came out of his hiding place slowly, his pointed head drooping unhappily. He edged over to the twins and stood staring up at them with a pleading look in his eyes. "I'm truly sorry, twins. Please, please forgive me," he bleated.

Debra's anger melted away, and her left dimple appeared.

David's anger melted away and his right dimple appeared.

"How can you be angry with a little goat who looks so sorry for all the mischief he has done?" David asked.

"This is Yom Kippur evening," said Debra, "and we're supposed to forgive everyone on Yom Kippur." Debra leaned down to give her little goat a tight bear hug. "I forgive you, G'dee. But you must try to be better." G'dee wagged his tail.

"I forgive you, too," said David, and he gave G'dee an even tighter bear hug. G'dee wagged his tail again. The sun was beaming once more.

Joseph tried hard to smile at the twins and their goat, but he couldn't help worrying about what Mr. and Mrs. Mann would say about the damaged lamp.

"I've been thinking," said David, "tonight is Yom Kippur evening. Let's ask God to forgive G'dee for all his mischief. Goats can't talk, and I'm sure G'dee would like to ask God to forgive him if he could."

Debra agreed with her usual enthusiasm. "That's a wonderful idea."

They tapped their foreheads thoughtfully. They had to think back a long way.

"Now let me see. What mischief shall we ask God to forgive first? I have it! Daddy's prize tulip bulbs—G'dee dug them up after Daddy planted them, and swallowed them whole."

"I've a good one. Your panda, Debra. G'dee chewed it until Panda's insides were all over the bedroom floor."

Joseph relaxed in a comfortable chair with his feet outstretched. This was going to take a long time.

"For eating the blueberry pie that Mother baked to serve to her club ladies," said Debra.

"For tangling himself in the yarn of the sweater Mother was knitting for Daddy," chuckled David. "Remember how furious G'dee was? Mother had to cut the yarn because G'dee was snarled up in such a hopeless tangle."

"I've thought of one!" interrupted Joseph, getting into the Yom Kippur spirit of forgiveness. "G'dee butted me while I was mowing your front lawn and made me fall flat on my face." Joseph glared at G'dee, remembering the embarrassment.

"For pulling the clothes off the clothes-line," said Debra.

"For eating the goldfish in the fish bowl," said David.

G'dee's naughty deeds were coming fast and furiously now. He ran to David, and to Debra, and back to David again. "Why bring up my dishonorable past? Let's look to the future! What's done is done!" he bleated. But it did no good—no good whatsoever. Stretching out on the floor, he decided to relax too. This was going to be a long drawn-out session. He was a goat that mischief followed everywhere.

"For chewing the knobs off the television set," said Debra. G'dee rolled his tongue around in his mouth. He could still feel the splinters.

"For biting the tire on Daddy's car so that Daddy had a flat tire on Beacon Street, right in the middle of the five-o'clock-coming-home traffic," said David. His left dimple flashed.

Debra whirled around on her tippety toes like a ballerina. "For spilling soap flakes on the broadloom carpet," she laughed. "It took a week to clean up that mess."

"For opening the bathtub faucet in the bathroom, and flooding the whole place," said David, imitating Debra's whirl, but not so gracefully.

Joseph interrupted again. "For nipping the postman every time he leaves the mail," he drawled.

"For frightening Tiger, the next-door cat, and cornering him on the fence," added David. "Poor Tiger is allergic to G'dee now. When G'dee comes anywhere near, Tiger bristles his whiskers and takes off faster than a shooting star."

David stopped short. Debra stopped short. They were breathless. Joseph looked at them. "Is that all?" he asked.

The twins ignored his question. Sure there were more, but these mischiefs were the most serious.

"Dear God, please forgive G'dee," pleaded Debra.

"Dear God, please forgive G'dee," pleaded David.

G'dee lifted his pointed head and looked at the twins. He ma-ma-a-a-a-ed at them and bowed his head. He was sorry. Really and truly he was sorry.

The front door opened and the twins heard Mother and Daddy come in. They ran to hug them. G'dee scooted like a guilty flash under the table.

"Oh, Mother, a perfectly dreadful thing has happened. But Joseph said it could be fixed, and David has $9.00 to pay for the damage. Please don't scold G'dee. It was an accident." Debra danced up and down, chattering away like a magpie.

"What's all this about?" asked Daddy.

Debra took Daddy by the hand. David took Mother by the hand. G'dee stayed under the table. Into the living-room they marched.

"My beautiful lamp," groaned Mother, covering her eyes with her hands.

"Where's that goat? I'll discombobulate him!" shouted Daddy, getting red in the face.

"Now Dad, don't get so excited. It was an accident. G'dee is sorry, honest he is—and Joseph said the lamp could be fixed," David tried to explain to Father.

"This is Yom Kippur evening, and you told us yourself that everybody should forgive everybody else on Yom Kippur. You did say that, didn't you?" Debra began to cry.

"Don't cry, honey," said Mother with a sigh. "It's only a lamp. Maybe it can be fixed. I know a man who is an expert at this sort of thing."

"Don't cry, Debra," said Daddy, wiping away her tears with his big handkerchief.

"Will you forgive G'dee? He'll be a good goat from now on, you'll see. Debra and I will watch him every minute, and we won't let him get into mischief any more. We promise. Don't we Debra?" David was pleading with all his heart. Debra took it from there.

"We asked God to forgive G'dee for all the wrongs he has done. Listen to the list." And before Mother and Daddy could say another word, David and Debra recited the long, long, long, list.

Daddy cleared his throat. "Well—well—" and he cleared his throat a second time. "I suppose—since it is Yom Kippur, I guess we must forgive G'dee."

With a joyful whoop the twins ran to hug G'dee under the table.

G'dee snuggled into them with a sigh of relief. That was a pretty serious discussion, and he *had* been worried while his fate hung in the balance.

"I love this Mann family, and best of all I love the twins," he ma-a-a-ed, as he winked at Joseph, who seemed to have

34

lost his tongue altogether. Debra's poem for Yom Kippur was just right.

> Dear God, please forgive,
> Forgive us this day.
> And keep us from harm,
> We earnestly pray.

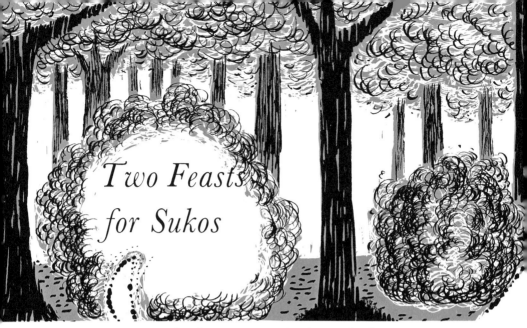

Two Feasts for Sukos

On Sukos those who know the best
Will point the lulov east and west.
To north and south, to earth and sky,
To show that God is always nigh.

Debra chanted her poem as the car sped smoothly over the country road. Debra and David and Daddy and G'dee were winging their way to the Blue Hills to gather branches to decorate the walls and cover the roof of the Temple Israel suko. Behind the school, in the garden, the carpenters had built a suko. On Sukos Day the children were going to have a party. How they looked forward to the Sukos fun.

Mr. Mann spied a good place to stop the car. They piled out. Into the woods they tramped until they came to a mossy carpet. Huge branches were everywhere. Soon they were gathering great heaps of fragrant branches, and carrying them to the car. When the back of the car was full Daddy opened the trunk, and used that space too.

G'dee was helping too. David thrust a branch into G'dee's mouth.

"Here, G'dee, take this to the car, please." Off scampered G'dee with the branch held firmly in his mouth. He was back in a few minutes. Debra did the same thing. G'dee liked

this game. It was such good fun. He was being an obedient goat. He was anxious to please his family, especially Daddy.

Everything was fine until—whisk! A bushy-tailed squirrel scooted suddenly in front of G'dee, frightening him within an inch of his goat life. G'dee's ears stood up like Indian wigwams. His whiskers flew up like a shelf. His mouth opened and the branch fell out. With a quick leap he was after the squirrel. No whisky, frisky squirrel was going to insult him!

He almost had the squirrel by the tail when it scampered up a tall tree—up, up, up, to the tippety top branch. There it sat toasting its tail in the sun, staring boldly down at G'dee.

G'dee tried to climb the tree. My—how he tried. But the bark was too slippery for him. Patiently he stood at the foot of the tree, glaring at his enemy, waiting for the squirrel to come down again. But Bushy Tail frisked through the sunny branches chattering away to the sky. G'dee waited and waited and waited. He was going to catch that scoundrel if it took all day and night.

Meanwhile, the twins and Daddy filled every bit of space in the car with spicy branches. They looked around for G'dee.

"G'dee," shouted Debra, "we're ready to go home."

"Now where could he have disappeared?" worried David.

"Ma-a-a-a-a," came an angry bleat from the direction of a tall tree. What a relief to find their goat safe! They coaxed and coaxed him to come with them, but the goat wouldn't budge. David and Debra couldn't understand G'dee's stubbornness. He had been so helpful all day.

"Let me be," bleated G'dee, "I'm going to teach that squirrel a lesson he'll never forget!"

Finally, David grasped G'dee by the right horn, and Debra grasped him by the left horn. Tugging at him with all their might, they dragged the unwilling goat to the car.

But when G'dee saw those tempting branches he forgot to be cross. Nestling in the soft branches he had the time of his goat life munching away. It was a feast fit for a crown prince, that is, a crown prince goat.

And that was G'dee's Sukos feast—number one.

The next day dawned crisp and clear. After school Mrs. Mann picked up the twins in the car. They were going to the temple suko to help decorate it. She drove them home quickly for some milk and cookies. When they came out to get into the car again, G'dee was waiting. The twins looked wistfully at Mother. G'dee looked wistfully at Mother. Mrs. Mann put them out of their suspense with a smile.

"All right, put G'dee in the back of the car, and hurry. We're late already. I do hope G'dee behaves himself."

G'dee nodded his head up and down. "Why do you always put ideas into my head?" he bleated, as the twins pushed him into the car.

When they arrived they found five mothers inside the

suko. Susan and Jonathan, classmates of the twins, were there too. When they saw G'dee they rushed over to hug him. G'dee felt very important.

The twins looked at the long tables. They saw shiny peppers and fat stringbeans and curly yellow squashes. They saw red twinkly apples and green sickle pears and bunches of deep purple grapes. On the walls and over the roof the mothers had already hung the spicy branches. How fragrantly everything smelled!

"It's like an enchanted forest," said Debra.

The mothers hung the fruit and vegetables among the branches. Mr. Kirkman was up on a tall ladder hanging fruit and vegetables on the branches in the highest part of the suko.

"How would you four children like to string these cranberries on this string?" asked Mrs. Mann, pointing to a pile of cranberries on the table.

David and Jonathan bored the holes with thick needles. Debra and Susan threaded the juicy berries on the long strings. G'dee was running about everywhere. He stood close to Debra, as close as close could be. Pop! Into his mouth slid a cranberry. He ran to Susan. Pop! Into his mouth went another cranberry. Another and another and another— the fruit flew into G'dee's mouth faster than it went onto the string. His beard was streaked with red juice. Some of the juice stained his face in spots.

"Look!" said Debra, "G'dee has the measles!" But G'dee didn't let that bother him. He was having a cranberry good time.

When the cranberry strings were threaded, Mr. Kirkman hung them in loops on the beams running across the ceiling, high, high up in the suko. G'dee kept glancing up at the delicious berries so far out of his reach. How he longed to be able to reach them. But how?

Debra looked up to the holes in the roof where the boards separated.

"Mother, why are the holes there?"

Mother smiled at her. "Our ancestors wandered about the desert for forty years, living in small huts called sukos, before they became a free nation. These huts were not their real homes. They could be swept away with a sudden gust of wind, and no longer shelter them. But our ancestors felt safe because they knew God was helping them. They felt protected no matter what happened. Today we leave holes in our suko roof to remind us that God is still near us."

Jonathan had something to add to Mother's story. "When they came to the Promised Land, our ancestors lived in sukos, too. They lived in them while they gathered in the harvest."

David had a question too. "Why do we hang fruits and vegetables in the suko?"

"The fruit and vegetables are God's gifts to all of us. This is how we show our thanks to God for everything He gives to us," said Mother.

David remembered about the Pilgrims. "Our teacher told us that the Pilgrims took their idea for Thanksgiving from our holiday of Sukos. Our ancestors celebrated Sukos by bringing the finest fruits and vegetables of the harvest to the Temple in Jerusalem."

Debra thought of a poem.

Gather in our suko cosy,
Hung with grapes and apples rosy,
Pretty flowers gayly spread,
Leafy branches overhead.

Thanking God we pray together·
For our blessings day by day,
Here in sunny autumn weather,
In our suko bright and gay.

Everybody clapped. Debra blushed. David was so proud he almost burst. Mrs. Mann just beamed all over.

"My uncle Joseph who lives in the State of Israel sent us a lulov and an esrog," said Debra, changing the subject. "The lulov is a sheaf of palm leaves tied together with three twigs of myrtle, and two branches of willow. All these trees grow in Uncle Joseph's garden. He has an esrog tree too."

Jonathan's mother asked, "Why do you suppose they chose those special trees?"

All the children were ready with the answer. They had studied it in religious school.

Jonathan said, "Miss Baron said it happened so long ago that no one really knows. But the rabbis said the lulov reminds us of the kings and prophets in the Bible."

"The myrtle reminds us of the wisdom of the Torah," said Susan.

"The drooping willow reminds us of the years our ancestors wandered over the face of the earth," said David.

"The esrog is the Jewish hope for the future," said Debra. All the mothers clapped again.

"I just love to hold the esrog close to my nose. It smells like French perfume," said Debra, closing her eyes and breathing in deeply.

David laughed and said, "Debra keeps sniffing. and sniffing at the esrog just like G'dee."

"Which reminds me, where is G'dee?" asked Debra, looking about the suko.

"He must have wandered into the garden," said David.

The children ran into the garden. They looked everywhere but G'dee was nowhere in sight.

"Ma-a-a-a," came an unhappy bleat from the top of the suko.

The children stared in amazement. Coming closer to the suko, David saw that G'dee had fallen into a hole in the roof, his front feet dangling inside. His hind feet were standing on a broad roof beam covered with branches. G'dee was wriggling the front of his body back and forth, but he couldn't budge his front legs.

"He must have climbed the ladder leaning at the side of the suko wall," thought David, wincing at his goat's cries of pain.

"I'll call Mr. Kirkman," said Debra, running inside the suko.

Mr. Kirkman and Debra came out, followed by all the mothers.

"Can you save my goat?" asked Debra. The lump in her throat was like a rock.

"Don't worry," promised Mr. Kirkman, "I'll figure something out." He climbed up on the ladder while the twins held it in place so that it wouldn't wobble. Everyone watched breathlessly.

Mr. Kirkman reached the roof. He saw that G'dee had fallen into a hole close to the side of the suko. With his long arms he leaned over and grasped G'dee's front legs where they joined his body. With a quick jerk he pushed G'dee straight up into the air. Pulling the trembling goat toward his chest, he came down the ladder. Placing G'dee on the grass, he wiped the beads of perspiration from his face. G'dee wobbled unsteadily.

"Oh, thank you, thank you," cried the twins, giving Mr. Kirkman a hug on both sides. The twins kneeled down and hugged G'dee, too.

"Thank Mr. Kirkman, G'dee," said Debra. Shaking his cranberry beard, G'dee tottered over to the janitor.

"Thank you for saving my life, Mr. Kirkman," he bleated, "those cranberries almost ruined me."

Mrs. Mann decided that her family had had enough excitement for one afternoon. She bundled them into the car. G'dee stretched himself out on the back seat. He yawned a great yawn, and fell asleep.

Mrs. Mann and the twins left him in the car when they arrived home. He slept in the car all night. And that was the end of G'dee's Sukos feast, number two.

Cinnamon Grass
for Simchas Torah

"DEBRA! DAVID! HERE'S A LETTER from Temple Israel for you," called Mrs. Mann.

The twins rushed up the playroom stairs, G'dee at their heels. In the letter was an unexpected and pleasant surprise.

> *Dear Debra and David:*
> On Tuesday, at the Simchas Torah services, the rabbi is going to bless all the children who have entered religious school for the first time. Afterwards, the mothers of the Sisterhood are having a Simchas Torah party for all the children, in the social hall. We want G'dee to come to the party, too. There will be a special surprise for your little goat.
>
> Affectionately,
> MRS. EDWARD JACOBSON
> *President of Sisterhood*

Debra danced around the room like a gay butterfly. David's grin was as wide as a jack-o'-lantern. They hugged G'dee.

"G'dee, you lucky goat. You're invited to a Simchas Torah party," said David.

G'dee wagged his stubby tail. He upped his nose in the

44

air and sniffed his best goat sniff. "Good food! Yummy-yum-yum!" he bleated. He somersaulted and rolled over the carpet.

An idea popped into Debra's head. "Come here, G'dee, come and be blessed." She beckoned to her little goat.

G'dee scooted under the chair. He didn't like the look in Debra's eye. She looked much too serious for his comfort. But Debra was determined. She ran after him, and dragged him out by the tail. "Face me, G'dee, and stand quietly," Debra's command was firm.

G'dee did as he was told. Pretending to be the rabbi, Debra placed her hands over G'dee's soft head, and murmured, "Echod, sh'nayim, sh'losho, arbo-o, chamisho," Debra didn't know the exact Hebrew words for the Consecration blessing, but she did know the Hebrew words for one, two, three, four and five. David chuckled and chimed in with Debra. "Echod, sh'nayim, sh'losho, arbo-o, chamisho," chanted the twins again, looking tenderly at their little pet.

"I like those strange words," bleated G'dee, licking his beard. "Somehow or other they make me feel like a good goat."

45

The night before the big day, the twins gave G'dee his Simchas Torah bath. They used Mother's perfumed soap because they wanted G'dee to smell good. They scrubbed and scrubbed until G'dee's coat was gleaming white.

When they came to G'dee's ears, he balked just like David always did. He wriggled in their grasp like a slippery, soapy eel.

"This is the washingest place," he bleated as the suds skidded into his eyes. "Scrub-a-dub-dub! Scrub-a-dub-dub! I'll be lucky if I get out of this with a whole skin. Quit it, twins! I hurt all over. Enough is enough!"

Last of all Debra polished G'dee's horns with floor wax. They shone like gold. "Simchas Torah, Operation G'dee is finished. G'dee could pass an army inspection test," she announced.

In the bathroom everything was in shambles. The tile floor was wet. The towels were wetter, and the twins were the wettest. The bathroom looked as if a hurricane had swept through it. When Mrs. Mann saw her bathroom she wrung her hands.

"Operation G'dee is now completed," said David.

"Operation G'dee should be renamed," said Mrs. Mann, "it should be called Hurricane G'dee. Get this place mopped up, my wet pets, or else—"

"Don't worry, Mother," interrupted David, "we'll clean up the mess."

They kept their promise to Mother's satisfaction.

Grandfather Mann came in. He had good news.

"The three generations of the Mann family, you, David, your father, and myself, have been honored by the temple," said Grandfather. "We have been chosen to carry the Torah Scrolls around the temple on Simchas Torah." The family beamed with pride.

They slept very little that night. G'dee snored louder than ever. Nothing ever interfered with his beauty sleep.

When they arrived at the temple the next morning, the twins led G'dee downstairs to the social hall. Mr. Kirkman greeted them with a welcoming smile. G'dee leaped up at the rosy-faced custodian, and licked his face. He hadn't forgotten Mr. Kirkman's kindness on the suko roof. G'dee didn't balk a bit when the twins left him to go to the services upstairs.

On the altar they saw the huge suko which had remained standing there since the Sukos services. Two solid, green-branched walls stretched forward from the Holy Ark to the front of the altar. In front of the altar the walls formed a giant picture frame through which the twins could see the white marble pulpit. Behind the pulpit against the rear wall were the polished doors of the Holy Ark where the Torahs were kept.

"Let's go down front and get a closer look at the suko," said Debra, pulling David by the hand.

"It's a good thing that G'dee isn't here. We'd have trouble keeping his curious nose out of all this good food," said David, as they came close to the suko.

Debra squealed. "Oh, how wonderful! Look," Debra pointed to some baskets overflowing with crab apples and pears and juicy grapes. They saw great blue hydrangeas and Japanese lanterns and red sprays of bittersweet interwoven among the branches. Ears of yellow and red corn marched up and down in rows, their corn silk peeping out of their coats. Debra looked at the great shasta daisies with laughing yellow centers.

"Look, David, they aren't daisies at all. The yellow centers are velvety lemons, and the petals are marshmallows tied around the lemons with a string."

David laughed and pointed to the giant pumpkins, like moons. They stroked the sunshiny squashes with curly burly skins. They looked up at the ceiling. Suspended from the ceiling was a red electric light casting a rosy holiday glow over the shining abundance.

"It's a Simchas Torah fairyland," said Debra, with shining eyes.

Daddy and Grandfather came to get David. They went into the rabbi's study. Debra took her seat beside mother and grandmother. The temple filled with excited children and their parents. Just before the services started Debra saw the rabbi, Grandfather, Daddy, and David come out on the pulpit. They sat down in the carved armchairs along the wall. David sat next to the rabbi.

When the organ sounded the services began. David felt very grown-up as he said the responses. The rabbi squeezed his arm, and smiled down at him. At last—at last—the great moment arrived. David's heart beat like a sledge hammer. He could hear the steady pounding from deep within him. He glanced at Daddy and Grandfather. They gave him big grins of encouragement.

Rabbi Israel opened the polished doors of the Holy Ark. Looking at the Torahs inside, the rabbi said, "Ho-vu

48

go-del la-lo-ha-nu, oo s'nu cho-vod la Torah. Let us declare the greatness of God and give honor to the Torah."

From the ark the rabbi took a Torah. He handed it to Grandfather. "As I hand this Torah to you I remind you of your duty to teach its wisdom to your son," said the rabbi.

From the ark the rabbi took another Torah which he gave to Daddy. "As I hand this Torah to you I remind you of your duty to teach its wisdom to your son."

Again from the ark the rabbi took another Torah. He handed it to David. David hugged it close and smiled shyly at the rabbi. Rabbi Israel said, "You, David, are the youngest in your family. When you are a man you will also teach the wisdom of the Torah to your son. Thus has the study of Torah been handed down from generation to generation. So will the Torah continue to be our Jewish way of life."

The rabbi took a Torah for himself. Facing the congregation, he said, "One of the most joyous ceremonies we have on Simchas Torah is Hakofos which means 'circling around.' When we parade around the temple we remember the wanderings of our people. We hope that the spirit of Torah will spread peace and justice throughout the world."

Holding the Torahs aloft, the three men of the family, with the rabbi leading the procession, stepped off the altar and marched down the right aisle. Around the temple they paraded. The children near the aisle reached out and touched the Torahs lovingly. The children who couldn't reach the Torahs blew kisses at the old scrolls. David hugged his Torah tenderly. His heart swelled up with love and his spine tingled. He had never felt so happy in his whole life.

When he passed the women in his family he grinned. Debra reached out and quickly placed a kiss on David's cheek. David's face flamed red with embarrassment. Debra gurgled at his discomfort.

49

Around the temple they marched and back up to the altar. Grandfather and Daddy returned their Torahs to the Holy Ark. David gave his Torah to the rabbi because the rabbi was going to read from it. Grandfather helped remove the cover, and Daddy said the blessing before reading the Torah. The rabbi unrolled the old parchment, and pointed to the sacred words with a carved silver pointer. Before he began to read the portion of the week he stopped to explain.

"Today we are joyful because we have the Torah. Every week during the year we read a portion of the Five Books of Moses. On Simchas Torah we come to the very last chapter. When we come to the last word we immediately begin all over again with the first word in Genesis. You see, the study of our wonderful Torah never really ends for the Jews. Listen carefully, children, and you will hear the last word and the first word. The last word is *Yisroel* which means 'Israel' and the first word is *B'rayshis,* which means 'in the beginning.' "

When David and Debra heard B'rayshis they smiled at each other. Rabbi Israel finished reading the Hebrew words and translated them so that everyone could understand.

The twins listened intently. Here in the temple they could see the beauty of the Torah with their own eyes, and listen to its wisdom with their own ears.

Rabbi Israel continued, "If we know and obey the words in the Torah we will lead good and useful lives."

Now Grandfather helped put the cover on the Torah, and Daddy said the blessing after the Torah. David helped the rabbi return the Torah to the ark.

The organ played and the rear doors opened slowly. Down the right aisle came twenty little girls, each carrying a small Torah dressed in a white velvet cover. At the same time twenty little boys came down the left aisle dressed in blue suits. They, too, carried small Torahs, dressed in purple velvet. They held their Torahs high for all to see. Right, left—right, left, they marched in time to the music. Debra laughed at one little girl who forgot to march slowly, and began to skip, her blonde pony-tail bobbing merrily behind her.

Up to the altar paraded the children. The rabbi was waiting for them under the glowing light, close to the still open ark. They crowded around the rabbi, quietly bowing their heads. He stretched his hands over the heads of the silent children. In a gentle loving voice he said the ancient blessing of consecration.

> Y'vorech'cho Adonoi v'yishm'recho.
> Yoer Adonoi ponov elecho v'chuneko.
> Yiso Adonoi ponov elecho v'yosem l'cho
>   sholom.

51

He translated the Hebrew words into English.

> May the Lord bless thee and keep thee,
> May the Lord let His countenance shine upon
>   thee, and be gracious unto thee,
> May the Lord lift up His countenance upon thee
>   and give thee peace.

The organ in the choir loft chanted a soft Amen. The little children sang the prayer they had learned in religious school with clear piping voices.

> Sh'ma Yisroel Adonoi Elohenu, Adonoi Echod,
> Hear O Israel, the Lord Our God, the Lord is
>   one.

The Consecration Service was over. Down the altar steps tripped the children to sit in the seats reserved for them.

Mother nudged Debra and whispered, "You'd better go downstairs, Debra, and see if G'dee is behaving himself."

Quietly Debra rose and tiptoed outside. Down to the social hall she danced on fairy wings, her face bright as a shining star. When G'dee spied her, he scampered over.

"Hi, Debra," he bleated, "glad to see you. Sorry I can't stay, I'm too busy helping with Simchas Torah." With a happy bleat he bounded away. He was too busy following the ladies of the Sisterhood. From the social hall to the kitchen he trotted, and from the kitchen to the social hall. So far he had managed to wangle six cookies, seven grapes, and eight dates.

Debra was ashamed of G'dee's greediness. She dragged him by the horn to the far end of the hall, as far away from the food as she could get. G'dee cast a disappointed eye at the long table heaped with Simchas Torah goodies. But he didn't dare disobey Debra's command.

After the services the children trooped down to the

social hall. David hurried over to Debra and G'dee. When the children saw the surprise goat they crowded around.

"G'dee," they shouted over and over again with excited voices. G'dee felt very special. He bowed his pointed head until his beard swept the floor.

The rabbi pushed his way through the crowd of children and stood in front of the twins and G'dee. "Welcome to our Simchas Torah party, G'dee," he chuckled as he held out a hand. G'dee didn't hesitate. Up came his right paw. Into the rabbi's outstretched hand it slipped. G'dee knew his social hall manners. "Thank you, Rabbi. Glad to be present," he ma-a-a-ed, wagging his tail.

And then came the promised surprise. Two Sisterhood mothers appeared carrying a huge basket. They set the basket on the floor in front of the goat. Inside G'dee saw sweet fresh grass sprinkled thickly with crisp, brown cinnamon sugar. It looked like a scrumptious feast. It smelled like a scrumptious feast. It tasted even better.

G'dee ate and he ate and he ate some more. When he finally came up for air his straggly beard was frosted with cinnamon sugar. The watching children shrieked with laughter.

Debra's new poem tumbled out of her mouth in a gay bubbling tune.

> Nothing at all can surpass
> Simchas Torah and cinnamon grass.
> You're a cinnamon goat, my darling G'dee,
> I'm glad you belong to David and me.

G'dee cocked his cinnamon beard at Debra. "You are so right, my dear," he bleated, licking his streaked beard with smacking lips.

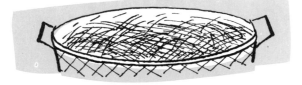

Plans for
Chanuko

IT WAS A FEW DAYS BEFORE CHAN-
uko. The family was in the living-room. Mother was unravel-
ing a skein of bright red yarn. G'dee was helping her. The
skein of yarn was stretched across G'dee's two horns, and he
was standing in front of Mother. He moved his horns this
way and that so that the wool could slip off easily. He cocked

54

his head and bleated, "How am I doing? Pretty smart for a goat, don't you think?"

Debra was chewing thoughtfully on her pencil. She was writing a poem for Chanuko. Father was decorating the living-room in honor of Chanuko. David was cutting out the menorahs that he and Debra had colored, and Daddy was sticking the menorahs on the giant picture window in the front of the living-room.

Debra put down her pencil with a sigh of relief. "There, I'm finished. Mother, would you like to hear my new poem?"

"Of course, darling," replied Mother, as she finished rolling the ball of yarn. She gave G'dee a thank-you pat on the back for being so helpful.

Debra recited her poem like an actress on television.

> Why am I so happy?
> Why am I so gay?
> Chanuko is coming,
> Joyous holiday.
> I'll clean my brass menorah,
> Shine it bright as gold,
> Hear about the Maccabees,
> Heroes brave and bold.

Mother gave Debra a hug. "I love your poem, dear. It sounds as if you really love Chanuko."

G'dee leaped over to Debra and nuzzled his head into her legs. He liked the poem too.

"Debra, how about a little help with these menorahs?" asked David. "On the double," laughed Debra, picking up a scissors and a menorah.

Soon the picture window gleamed with gay menorahs. Grabbing their coats, the twins ran outdoors to see how they looked from the outside.

Debra clapped her hands with delight. "Those menorahs make our home look happy and safe."

"Just think, Debra, in olden days Antiochus, the Greek king, refused to allow the Jews to celebrate their holidays."

"That mean old Antiochus put an idol of Jupiter in the Holy Temple in Jerusalem, and commanded the Jews to bow down to it. Would you have obeyed him, David? I wouldn't."

David laughed at Debra's question. "I'm glad I live in America where we are free, and can have menorahs in the windows. But I'll tell you this, Debra. If I'd been living then, I'd have been a soldier in Judah Maccabee's army. That's for sure! I would fight for right with might!" David lunged at Debra with a make-believe sword in his right hand.

"That's a poem, David, fight for right with might. Look, there's G'dee at the window licking a menorah!"

They ran back into the house laughing. G'dee bounded over to them and bleated, "Why didn't you take me?" Debra patted him to soothe his hurt feelings.

They saw that Mother and Daddy had strung a long string in front of the fireplace. Swinging from the string were huge sparkling blue letters. The dancing letters spelled: Happy Chanuko.

"How beautiful," said Debra. "Just what we need to brighten up our Maccabees on the fireplace shelf." Debra looked at the clay statue of Mattathias she had made in religious school. On the statue she had painted a blue robe, and a long white beard. Mattathias was very shiny because he had two coats of shellac. "Wise old Mattathias, how proud you must have been of your five sons." Debra patted the statue on the shoulder.

David looked happily at the clay statue he had molded of Judah Maccabee, his favorite hero. Judah wore a short tunic with red and blue stripes. On his head was a silver painted helmet, and in his hand was a silver sword. "Judah seems so real to me." David stroked the tiny sword. "I can almost hear him shouting to his soldiers, 'Follow me! On to victory!'" David's heart overflowed with love and admiration for his hero.

"David, do you know something? We ought to have the rest of the brothers of the Maccabean family to make it complete."

"That's a good idea, let's make them tomorrow."

"Do you have enough clay?" asked Mother.

"If you don't, I'll bring some home tomorrow," said Daddy. "What are the other brothers' names, David? I've forgotten."

"Wait a minute, Daddy. Our religious school teacher gave us some poems about the Maccabees for our notebooks. I'll get them in a jiffy." David ran out of the room. He was back in three shakes of a goat's tail.

"Let me help you read them, David?" asked Debra.

"You read one and then I'll read one. All right?"

The twins stood near the mantelpiece. Mother and Daddy looked proudly at them. G'dee was licking a menorah on the window.

David read the first one.

57

Jochanan walked gently
Wherever he trod,
Jochanan loved Torah
Lived closely to God.

Debra read the second one.

Eliezar the giant
Had power and might,
With the strength of Samson
He carried the fight.

David went on.

Youngest was Jonathan
A lad but half-grown,
Eager his willingness,
A daring his own.

Debra took the paper.

Simon was the plain one,
A loyal friend in need,
Simon gave them courage
With every noble deed.

"And now for the best brother of all," said David, looking fondly at his clay statue.

The greatest one was Judah,
A leader of his men,
He knew his holy purpose.
He had the strength of ten.
To battle-field they followed,
Yearning to be free.
With faith in God he led them,
Judah Maccabee.

They were out of breath when they finished. Mother and Daddy clapped.

"I like Jonathan. He was the youngest, but he could climb like a goat over the cliffs, and spy out the enemy," said Debra.

58

G'dee perked up his ears at the mention of the word, goat. He leaped onto the divan. "I'm as good a climber as that Jonathan, any day," he bleated, heading for the top of the divan's back.

"Oh, no, you don't." Daddy lifted G'dee off the divan and put him on the floor. G'dee nipped Daddy's trousers, and Daddy spanked him on the tail.

Mrs. Mann had an idea. "How would you like to have a Chanuko party, twins?" she asked.

"Mother!" squealed Debra, whirling around like a pinwheel.

"What a stupendous idea!" shouted David, jumping up and down.

He jumped so hard Judah Maccabee toppled right off the fireplace. It was a lucky thing that Daddy was standing close enough to the mantel. He caught Judah with his right hand just like a baseball pitcher.

"Take it easy, son," Daddy put Judah back on the mantel. G'dee waggled his ears, and his beard, and his tail, all at the same time. "I love parties," he ma-a-a-ed at all of them, "good things to eat and eat and eat. What more can a goat with my appetite ask?"

"Mother, can we make it a Chanuko masquerade party?" asked Debra, laughing at G'dee. "Why not?" laughed Mother.

"What will I wear?" asked Debra, wrinkling her forehead. "What will I wear?" asked David, wrinkling his forehead. Their faces lit up like neon lights. They both thought of a costume at the very same time.

David announced, "I'll be Judah Maccabee."

Debra announced, "I'll be Mrs. Judah Maccabee."

Daddy and Mother and David exploded with laughter.

"Did Judah Maccabee have a wife? I've never heard a wife mentioned," said Daddy, winking at Mother.

"I've never heard that he didn't have a wife. Anyway he was so brave and handsome he must have had one." Debra looked at them with a determined expression on her face.

"Of course, you can be Mrs. Maccabee, dear," said Mother. "Stop teasing her, Daddy."

"And how will G'dee be dressed? As Judah Maccabee's horse, no doubt?" Daddy couldn't resist that remark.

David burst out with a whoop. "Dad, you're a genius! I was wondering about G'dee's costume. He'll make a wonderful horse for Judah Maccabee!"

Daddy was flabbergasted. He had only been joking when he had suggested that idea.

Everyone talked at once after that. There was so much to decide. What would Judah Maccabee wear? What would Mrs. Judah Maccabee wear? What would Judah's horse wear? Refreshments? Entertainment? Games? Prizes? The air was full of excited voices. G'dee ran from one to the other, but he was ignored completely. He couldn't understand such goings-on. In disgust, he scooted under the piano, and covered his ears with his paws.

The twins wrote the invitations with Mother's help. This is what the letter to Jonathan said:

> *Dear Jonathan:*
> Would you like to come to our party on the first night of Chanuko? Come at seven o'clock in the evening. Please wear a costume. The costume must have something to do with Chanuko. There will be prizes, for the best costume.
> Your playmates,
DEBRA and DAVID MANN

When the invitations were ready, David called G'dee to lick the stamps. G'dee felt better right away. The glue was delicious.

Out to the mail-box ran David, with G'dee at his heels. Debra danced around the room, singing a gay tune.

> Why am I so joyful?
> Yes, why am I so gay?
> Chanuko is coming,
> A party's on the way.
> I know that Mother and Daddy
> Are planning a heap of fun.
> It seems to take forever
> Till Chanuko's begun.

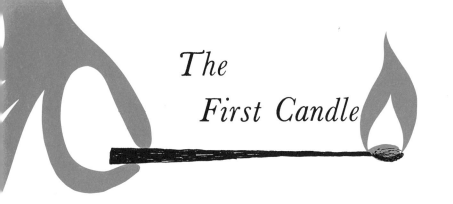

The First Candle

DAVID AND DEBRA AND G'DEE FOL-
lowed their noses into the kitchen on the morning of the first
day of Chanuko. On the table was a huge round cake covered
with thick orange frosting. Beside the cake on a huge platter
were tall ginger-bread men with orange collars. Fat brown
raisins marched in a straight line down their frosted coats.
G'dee licked his lips and edged over to the table very, very
slowly.

But—David was alert and grabbed G'dee just in time.

"Not this time, you don't. You'll wait until the party,
just like the rest of us." David dragged G'dee out back to
give him his breakfast of sweet grass.

G'dee looked at the grass and then looked at David. His
look said very plainly, "I'd like it much better if this grass
had some thick orange frosting on it."

At ten o'clock the door bell rang. A delivery man handed
Mrs. Mann a large square package. The return address told
them that the package had been sent by Uncle Joseph from

the State of Israel. It was a shiny menorah, the most beautiful menorah the twins had ever seen. Uncle Joseph had sent it just in time for Chanuko. There was a letter in the package, too, addressed to the twins.

The menorah was brass, painted a deep chocolate brown. On the broad base were eight candleholders. The shamos holder was on a high pedestal held up in back by two carved lions standing on their hind legs. First, Debra held the menorah carefully. Then, David held it carefully. The menorah was heavier than it looked. They decided to put it on the mantel in the center of the Maccabee family that they had made. How beautiful it looked gleaming proudly on the shelf.

"My Uncle Joseph thinks of the most wonderful gifts to send, first G'dee and now the menorah," said David.

"He's my Uncle Joseph, too," said Debra. "Mother, let's read the letter."

Mother read the letter with the twins looking over her shoulder.

Dear Debra and David:

I wish you could be in Tel Aviv during the joyous Chanuko season. If you were Israeli children you would take part in the Candle-Light Parade. In the late afternoon the children march to a large open field on the outskirts of the city, each one holding a small menorah. Here they wait for a signal. A voice booms over a loud-speaker.

"Go forth, children, with this fire and kindle faith and courage in your hearts as did the Maccabees of old!" The children then light their menorahs, and hold them high in the air. The open field turns into a flaming island lighting up the darkness for miles around. Swinging their menorahs in time to joyful Chanuko songs, the children march homeward. In the city high above the roof tops of the houses, on top of the Great Synagogue, the children are greeted with a giant menorah lighting up the sky.

I hope that both of you will enjoy Chanuko and this menorah.

Your loving uncle,
JOSEPH

David and Debra were breathless with wonder.

"Some day I'd like to really be in that candle parade," said Debra, with shining eyes.

"Me too," agreed David.

"I'll put the letter here on the mantelpiece where Daddy can read it," Mother said. "And now my darling twins, there's work to be done! Scoot!"

64

David and Debra wrapped their gifts in the Chanuko paper that Mother had bought at the temple gift shop. David's paper was sprinkled with dancing red and blue dreidels. Debra's paper was covered with shiny yellow menorahs. They tied the gay packages with blue and gold ribbon and heaped them on top of the piano. Mother and Daddy put their presents there, too.

It was so hard for the twins to wait until the lighting of the menorah before they could open their gifts. G'dee had several gifts, too. One of the presents was on the floor. He sniffed and sniffed. "Ma-a-a-a," it smelled good to his goat nose.

At sunset the family gathered in the gaily decorated living-room. Grandmother and Grandfather Mann were there, too. Their eyes glowed with happiness. Mother took the menorah down from the mantel and placed it on the coffee table where the twins could reach it easily. Grandfather stuck a candle in the first holder. Grandmother stuck a candle into the shamos holder. Grandfather began, "The Maccabees fought the first war for religious freedom in all history. Even though they were few in number, they fought hard and God gave them a great victory. In honor of their courage we light the first candle of Chanuko."

David lit the shamos candle and handed it carefully to Debra. As Debra lit the first candle they sang the Chanuko

blessings. The sweet music of the ancient Chanuko blessings filled the room. They thanked God for allowing them to be together at this time, at this season. "Let's sing 'Rock of Ages' now," said David. G'dee gazed at them and he gazed at the gleaming menorah. His goat heart beat fast. "How lucky I am to be a part of this happy family on this joyful holiday," he bleated, blinking his eyes at the twin lights on the menorah.

"May we open our presents now?" asked David, impatiently.

"I'll burst if I have to wait another single minute," said Debra.

"Patience, my pets," chuckled Daddy, "these are your first night's presents. We have presents for you for every one of the eight days of Chanuko. Ready—on your mark—*go!*"

Such squeals of delight! There was a train set for David and an Israeli doll for Debra from their parents. There was a world globe that lit up by electricity for the twins from their grandparents. There were two books for the twins too. David's book was a picture book, about the State of Israel, and Debra's book was an illustrated Bible story book.

For G'dee, Mother had knitted a blue woolly blanket with G'DEE embroidered on it in red letters. There was a leather collar with G'DEE studded on it in brass nail-heads from Grandfather and Grandmother.

The biggest surprise of all was a huge box of oats from the children in the twins' religious school class. Mrs. Mann allowed G'dee to catch a faint whiff, and quickly hid the box in the storeroom closet. She didn't want her broadloom covered with oats. After all, they were having a party.

"I hate to interrupt these important proceedings," said Mother, "but isn't it time to dress for the party?"

"Oh, I almost forgot," said Debra, jumping to her feet.

"I guess we'd better hurry," said David with a last fond

look at the train set. "Come on, Dad, I need your help."

But Daddy didn't hear. He was busy examining the trains. David dragged him away. "I'll let you play with my trains, tomorrow," he promised with a giggle. Daddy followed David with a backward glance at the trains.

In a short while they were dressed. Debra wore a long white robe that Mother had made from a pair of old bedroom curtains. Around her waist was a red velvet sash tied into a pretty bow. Three long strings of pearls hung around her neck. Mother tucked a red rose into Debra's hair. She looked like an enchanted princess who had just stepped out of fairyland. Indeed, Debra was the perfect wife for Judah Maccabee.

The men in the family whistled long and loud when she paraded in front of them like a model.

David wore a short tunic with a skirt of blue and red stripes. Over his shoulder was a magnificent purple cape with the word MACCABEE pinned over the back in flaming red letters. A silver cardboard helmet with a tall red plume sat on his head, and at his side was a scabbard holding a real sword. When Debra saw him, she dimpled up at him. "What a handsome husband I have!" she giggled.

"Follow me—my brave Maccabees—and I shall lead you to victory!" commanded David, brandishing his sword at his wife.

And now, it was time to dress Judah Maccabee's horse. But the about-to-be-converted horse had vanished. Everyone called for G'dee but no goat appeared. In the hall David spied G'dee's tail sticking out of the half-shut storeroom closet. The tail was switching back and forth, back and forth. G'dee had discovered the box of oats. David tried to drag his goat out of the closet, but would that stubborn goat go?

Not on your life! He would fight to open that box of oats if it took a century and a half. His was the courage of a Maccabee.

David had a bright idea. He rushed into the kitchen and snatched up a gingerbread man. He held its tempting fragrance under G'dee's sensitive nose. It worked! G'dee backed out of the closet with the speed of a cannon-ball. He followed the gingerbread man into the living-room. David gave him the cake, and they set to work. When they were finished, G'dee was the strangest looking goat-horse that had ever been seen. He looked like a horse from outer space.

On each horn was a tiny silver helmet like David's. Around his neck and under his beard were silver reins with dangling silver bells that tinkled merrily when he moved. The very best part was his tail. Long orange crepe paper streamers hung to the floor, completely hiding his own perky tail. G'dee kept turning around to stare at his new tail. He cocked his head and bleated in disgust, "This is a tail? This is a horse? I'd rather be a goat, thank you!" He ran over to the mirror and flipped his tail so that he could see it. "If this is what I have to be—so be it," he bleated at the mirror.

G'dee was ready for the Chanuko party, orange tail and all.

Latkes!
Latkes!
Latkes!

THE FIRST GUEST TO ARRIVE WAS
Susan dressed as a Maccabean Hannah. She wore a long
pink robe with a flowered kerchief on her head. She came in
wheeling a baby carriage crowded with boy dolls. There were
seven of them to represent her seven sons. On the carriage
was a sign, DOWN WITH ANTIOCHUS!

Next to arrive was Wendy; she was a latke. Her tan
dress was covered with painted paper latkes. The latkes
looked so real that even G'dee was fooled. He ran over to
Wendy and began to eat what he thought was a latke. He
made a sour face when he discovered that it was paper.

The bell rang again, and in trooped Jonathan and
Lewis, as two Maccabees. When David saw them, he drew
his sword and shouted, "Copy cats, follow me. On to victory!" The three Maccabees had a mock battle on the spot.
Wendy and Susan and Debra shrieked at the top of their
voices, as they tried to duck the swords that were waving
wildly in the air.

In came Ronald spinning around in circles. He was a
dreidel in a clown suit. On his head was a red hat with four

sides. Each side had a different Hebrew letter painted on it. There was a *nun*, a *gimel*, a *shin*, and a *hay*. He spun into Debra, knocking the rose out of her hair.

G'dee picked up the rose in his mouth and lowered his horns. No one, not even a Chanuko dreidel, could do that to his Debra. He charged into Ronald knocking him to the floor. Mrs. Mann came to the rescue. She picked Ronald up and straightened his hat. "Did you get hurt?" she asked, feeling Ronald for any broken bones.

"I'm all right, Mrs. Mann. It's all in fun."

Linda came into the living-room. The children exclaimed when they saw her white and gold costume. She was a Chanuko fairy. A golden wand with a huge tinsel Jewish star on the top was in her hand. Her graceful wings were edged with glittering gold tinsel. The wings bumped into G'dee, who came over to inspect the shining fairy. On Linda's head was a golden crown.

Roger and Peter came in together. Roger was a funny clown with a white painted face. When Mrs. Mann saw him she said, "Roger, I didn't know that there were clowns in Maccabean days."

Roger grinned up at her with a twinkle, "I made the Maccabees laugh when they were weary with battle."

Peter was Mr. *Nes Godol Hoyo Shom,* the Chanuko Miracle Man. He wore a long orange coat with a pointed orange hat. He carried an orange wand in his hand that he kept waving at everyone. He pointed the wand at Debra. "I, Mr. Nes Godol Hoyo Shom, the Chanuko Miracle Man, do hereby command that you be changed into a pink cat with purple eyes!" said Peter.

Last to come in was Sara, the Spirit of Chanuko. She wore a snowy ballerina costume with tiny orange candles sewed all over the skirt. On her head was a white crown with candles sewed all over it, too. In her hand was a small golden menorah.

Mrs. Mann looked at Mr. Mann, and Mr. Mann looked at Mrs. Mann.

"Yes, dear, I know just what you are thinking." Daddy put on his coat. "I'll have to hop down to the store to pick up some more prizes. All of them deserve one. These costumes are wonderful!"

Grandfather added with a smile, "And I'll pay for them, son."

G'dee was a big hit. The children laughed and laughed at the tail. Roger pulled the orange streamers. G'dee ran away from him. But every time he ran, the pesky tail had a habit of getting in his way. What was he to do? His goat brain worked fast. "I know," he bleated. "I know just how to get around that problem." He kicked his hind legs upward as he ran, so that the streamer tail flew up into the air at the same time. He was beginning to feel almost like a horse.

He peered into Susan's doll carriage, but he walked away in disgust.

"Dolls," he bleated, "goats can't eat dolls!" With a flip of his paper tail he wandered over to inspect Sara.

"Ma-a-a-a," he bleated, nibbling at a candle.

"Get away, G'dee, you'll get sick," cried Sara, dancing up and down in alarm.

But G'dee paid no heed to Sara. He liked candles. They were delicious. Sara jumped up on the divan, and G'dee leaped up after her, nibbling on another candle. Grandfather came to the rescue. He lifted G'dee and banished him to the kitchen, closing the door after G'dee's sorrowful bleat.

It was time to play the Chanuko games.

"Time to pin the candle on the menorah," called Mother, as she taped an empty cardboard menorah on the wall. She explained the rules of the game. Each one had to be blindfolded. Whoever came closest to pinning the candle on the shamos holder would win a prize.

When Debra's turn came, David blindfolded her and gave her three quick spins. Instead of heading toward the menorah, Debra headed toward the kitchen. The children followed her out of the living-room very quietly, so that they wouldn't give away the joke. Debra walked slowly, feeling her way in the air with her hands. *Bump!* Smack into the kitchen door slammed her nose.

"Ouch!" she cried. When she saw where she had wandered, she laughed and rubbed her wounded nose.

"Mrs. Maccabee looks like she battled the Greeks," David touched his sister's red nose.

How the children laughed as they ran back to finish the game. David came closest to the shamos, but he gave the prize to Peter who was next.

Daddy returned with more prizes. Everyone received a wonderful game. Grandfather was next on the program. He was a magician with many tricks up his sleeve.

Mrs. Mann came into the room.

"Come and get it," she called, but the children didn't hear her. They were engrossed watching Grandfather. Their eyes were riveted on him with looks of wonder. Grandfather was pulling a cigarette out of Linda's ear.

Mrs. Mann picked up David's megaphone. *"Come and get it!"* she blared into the megaphone.

This time the children did hear. They rushed toward the closed dining-room. Mother opened the sliding doors. Everyone's eyes popped. G'dee was standing on the table. Nes Godol Hoyo Shom! A great miracle happened there! His right front foot was standing plunk in a mold of orange jello. His left front foot was standing plunk in the cake with orange frosting. His right hind foot was standing plunk in a plate of orange marmalade. And his left hind foot was standing plunk in a bowl of orange dahlias.

A thunderous roar of laughter rose up from the children. Mrs. Mann didn't know whether to laugh or cry. G'dee bleated crossly. He didn't see anything to laugh about. He was *standing* on all this delicious food, not *eating* it. How in the world was he going to crawl out of this mess, and still get some of this food he was standing on into his hungry stomach?

Daddy and Grandfather came toward him. They lifted G'dee off the table. *Poor G'dee!* He dripped with orange food. His eyes yearned toward the table as he was carried into the kitchen. Daddy washed his oozing feet at the sink. When he was finished, Daddy tied G'dee to the front door-knob with a leash.

"Stay there, you naughty goat," he said crossly, "enough is enough!"

Mother and Grandmother removed the spoiled food from the table. Luckily there were plenty of other things to eat. Grandmother came in bearing a platter of crisp brown latkes. The shouts of glee could be heard all the way to the moon. Latkes! Crisp golden brown latkes! This was a real Chanuko party.

David and Debra and Sara heaped cinnamon sugar on their latkes. Peter and Wendy and Linda spooned sour cream on theirs. Susan and Lewis and Jonathan chose applesauce. But Roger tried everything. Onto his latkes went the sour cream *and* the applesauce *and* the cinnamon sugar.

M-m-m-m-m-m-m-m-m-m-m-m-m-m- *delicious!*

Wendy held a piece of latke on her fork in midair. "When I decided to be a latke for the party, I found a lovely story about why we eat latkes on Chanuko."

Roger laughed. "Because they're good to eat, of course." He speared another latke.

Wendy laughed and looked at him as if he weren't there. "Yes, but that's no story, smarty. Once when the

Maccabees were chasing the Greeks, they passed through a small village. They asked the women of the village to feed them quickly because they were in a great rush. The women made the pancakes because this was the quickest food they knew how to make."

"Did they have cinnamon sugar and sour cream and applesauce in those days to heap on their pancakes?" asked Roger, winking at everyone.

"Oh, you!" laughed Wendy. "And anyway, even if they did have those things they wouldn't dare to eat all that at one time. They were fighting a war, remember? They couldn't afford to get tummy aches."

"Don't worry about my stomach," chuckled Roger, his mouth crammed with latke, "Mother says that it's made of iron."

Meanwhile, G'dee was straining at his leash. His orange tail was in shreds. One helmet had fallen off his horn into the sink, and the other helmet was hanging crazily half off the other horn. The bells on his reins were ringing angrily. The smell of the latkes was tantalizing and tormenting at the same time.

Suddenly Debra stood before him. She popped a latke into G'dee's open mouth. He gulped it down in one swallow and smacked his lips greedily.

"What are you waiting for? It's Chanuko and I want to eat latkes. More! More!" he bleated.

Debra hurried back to the dining-room. Out came David with two more latkes. G'dee was quicksilver as he gobbled them up. And then every five minutes out came, one by one, Sara and Peter and Susan and Wendy and Ronald and Jonathan and Lewis and Linda. All of them came laden with latkes for G'dee.

He ate and he ate and he ate until—the latkes were coming out of his ears and his eyes. He pushed the last two

pancakes away, wearily—very wearily. "If I don't see another latke as long as I live, I won't care. Honestly, I won't
care a bit!" he bleated with a drowsy sigh, and G'dee slipped
off into dreamland.

The lights in the dining-room went out. "Ladies and
gentlemen of Chanuko," said Grandfather, "lend me your
ears. Everyone must be silent. The great moment has arrived!"

The children wondered what was about to happen.
They were as quiet as the falling snow.

Grandfather continued. "After their great victory the
Maccabees returned to the Temple in Jerusalem. The first
thing they did was to clean the Temple. They destroyed all
the idols and made the Temple holy once more."

Grandfather twinkled at the silent children. "But, a
legend tells us, when they came to kindle the everlasting
light there was only oil to last for one day and one night—"

At that point Peter, the Chanuko Miracle Man, almost
fell off his chair. "That's my story, Mr. Mann. Please let
me tell the ending."

Grandfather stopped. "No one here has a better right to
tell it than you, Peter."

"It would have taken eight whole days and eight whole
nights to get more oil. But—Nes Godol Hoyo Shom—a
great miracle happened there—the oil lasted for eight nights
and eight days—and ever since that time the Jews have celebrated the glorious holiday of Chanuko for eight days."
Peter finished his story all in one breath.

Grandfather's voice was hushed and mysterious. "And
now—and now—wonderful miraculous things are about to
happen here!"

And then—and then—and then—it happened!

Grandmother wheeled in a serving table heaped with
the most wonderful ice cream that the children had ever seen.

Each ice cream was an orange dreidel with a lighted candle stuck in the top. Such oh's and ah's!

The twins served. After they **had** served their guests, they took their chairs.

"I'm going to count three," said Debra, "and when I say three, everyone make a Chanuko wish, and blow out the candle light. If you do exactly as I say, maybe the wish will come true."

Everyone waited breathlessly.

"One—Two—Three—Blow!"

They blew and they blew and they blew until every light was out. After that you couldn't hear a sound except the scrape of the spoons against the plates.

"Daddy, don't you think that G'dee has been punished enough?" asked David.

"All right, David, bring him in and we'll give him an ice cream dreidel."

But when they went to get G'dee they found him snoring in his beard. One paw was cuddled around a half-eaten latke. G'dee was away off in his goat dreamland, dreaming about dozens of latkes with dangling orange streamers, chasing him around a lighted Chanuko menorah, around . . . and around . . . and around . . . and around.

Parakeet Trouble

THE TWINS WERE IN THE PLAYROOM
building a tower with their blocks. Shalom, their new parakeet, was sitting on David's head watching the construction
project. Their grandparents had given them the bird a few
weeks ago as a surprise. When Debra saw the heavenly blue
bird for the first time, she cried, "Shalom, you pretty bird,"
and the parakeet's name became Shalom that very day.

The tower was growing taller and taller. The twins
carefully added block after block. "Let's try to reach the
ceiling," said Debra.

Suddenly Shalom swooped down and pushed a block at
the very bottom of the tower with his beak. Down came the
tower, peppering the twins with falling blocks.

"Ouch!" cried David, as two blocks hit him on the nose.

"Ouch!" cried Debra, as three blocks hit her on the
head.

"Squawk!" squawked Shalom, flying quickly to the flu-
orescent light hanging from the ceiling.

"Debra, David," called Mother from the kitchen, "lunch
is ready." Up the stairs scrambled the twins, Shalom flying
behind them.

80

While they were eating their lunch Shalom perched on the table, sampling the food. He darted here and he darted there. He thrust his sharp beak into some cream cheese. And then he tried to get it off. No success! He cocked a pleading look at Debra—and at David—and at Mother. No help whatsoever from that department! They waited to see what would happen.

Shalom flew over to Mother's coffee cup. He perched himself on the rim of the cup, and jabbed his cheesy beak into the hot coffee. The cream cheese slid off easily into the coffee. Shalom, very pleased with his cleverness, burst into a gay song. The twins were very happy with their new pet.

But not G'dee—he found nothing to be happy about. That Shalom was getting too much attention—attention that rightfully belonged to him. The twins were forever busy teaching Shalom new tricks. He couldn't understand why they were making such a fuss over a silly parakeet, anyway.

Debra stood in front of the cage saying, "Pretty bird," over and over again, and after a while Shalom said, "Pretty bird."

Debra was beside herself with joy. Now, what was so wonderful about that?

Then David, just as foolishly, stood in front of Shalom's cage and said, "David, David," over and over again, until finally—finally the stubborn bird said, "David." David grinned proudly—he was the proudest boy in the world. Now—what was so wonderful about that?

G'dee was disgusted. What a waste of good time! There were so many things that Shalom couldn't do. Could Shalom run about outside in the snow? No indeed! Parakeets are much, much too delicate. They catch cold so easily. Could Shalom eat garbage? No indeed! Parakeets must have extra special food. Could Shalom pull a cart? Impossible! That weak bird would collapse like a balloon with a pin in it.

If only he could catch that pesky bird—he'd put a stop to all this nonsense. But—and this really made him angry—Shalom always managed to escape G'dee's paws no matter how hard he tried to catch him. And to make matters worse, the bird just adored sitting on G'dee's back pecking him with sharp little pecks whenever he had the chance, which was too often—much too often to suit G'dee. And it hurt—it really hurt!

And that wasn't all that was wrong. The twins were in a play in religious school in honor of Tu Bi-Sh'vot, the New Year of the Trees. They were always busy memorizing their parts. Between the parakeet and the play, G'dee drooped with loneliness. He had nothing to do but chase his tail, and glare at Shalom as he flew about in the air, almost in his grasp, but never quite in his mouth.

G'dee was wrong, though. He was very much in the twins' thoughts. They proved that at religious school the next week.

Miss Baron, their teacher, announced that the Keren Ami money would be used to buy trees to plant in the State of Israel. On the bulletin board were many posters with huge trees printed on them. Each tree had twenty empty

spaces outlined. The outlines were shaped like leaves. The children bought leaves for ten cents apiece, and pasted the leaves in the empty spaces.

David and Debra had fifty cents each. They bought five leaves apiece. How happy they were to be able to paste so many leaves on the trees.

Mother had also given them four dollars to buy two trees to plant in memory of her parents who had died when the twins were babies. When the posters were filled the class had bought thirteen trees.

Miss Baron asked, "Why is it important to plant trees in the State of Israel?"

The twins waved their hands. "When you plant the trees you keep the soil from wearing out," said Debra, "and the trees keep the water in the ground, too." "Trees give the people shade and fruit and they make the country beautiful," said David.

Miss Baron turned to the blackboard. "In our daily prayer let us thank God for the beauties of nature. Who would like to read the prayer that I have written on the board?"

Vicki and Jonathan raised their hands, and Miss Baron told them to walk to the front of the room.

Vicki began, "We thank you, God, for the trees."

Jonathan finished, "Please care for the trees, O Lord, and help them to grow strong and tall."

Miss Baron told the children about her visit to the Union of American Hebrew Congregations' Forest in the State of Israel. "I was so surprised when I first saw the forest," said Miss Baron. "It wasn't like the forests of America at all. The trees were small and very young. But—in a few years these trees will grow tall and strong. Already they are beginning to change the face of the land. The care of these forests are in the hands of many of the new people who have come to live in Israel from the four corners of the world."

"I'm glad that we are helping to plant trees there," said Debra, "it makes me feel as if I were really helping the Jews there."

Miss Baron continued. "One of the loveliest customs in the olden days in Palestine shows how much the people loved trees. When a girl was born a cypress tree was planted, and when a boy was born a cedar tree was planted. The girls and boys tended their trees lovingly. Later when they grew up, and were married, the branches of their trees were cut down, to use as poles to hold up their wedding canopies.

Things moved along quickly that morning. At eleven o'clock the class trooped down to the auditorium for the rehearsal. All the children knew their parts perfectly. Their voices rang out loud and clear. You could hear them in the very last row. David opened his mouth so wide—that twenty chickens could roost inside. Debra opened her mouth so wide —that twenty chickens could roost inside. Miss Baron was pleased.

Suddenly Debra ran over to Miss Baron, her face burning with excitement. "Miss Baron, can G'dee be in our play?"

Miss Baron gasped at this unusual request. "Now what could G'dee possibly do in our Tu Bi-Sh'vot play, Debra? And if we did think of something for him to do, how can we be sure that G'dee would behave? There will be trees in the play, and you know how G'dee likes to eat—especially tender green trees."

Debra was determined. "If you find something for G'dee to do in the play, I'll think of some way to make G'dee behave. Please, Miss Baron, G'dee has never been in a play before. I just know that he'll make a wonderful actor."

All the children gathered around Miss Baron and Debra. They added their pleas to Debra's. "Please, please, please," they clamored.

The teacher put her hands to her ears, and motioned for silence.

"Well—now—that is an idea—and—perhaps—G'dee can pull a cart across the stage."

Debra hugged Miss Baron. "You're a peach, teach. David and I thank you from the bottom of our hearts."

"Now remember, Debra, you must be sure that G'dee doesn't eat those trees," warned Miss Baron, already half regretting her promise to turn G'dee into an actor. But how could she refuse Debra, who was always so helpful and willing? The teacher comforted herself with the thought that G'dee on the stage would be an unusual idea. She had never heard of a goat on the stage before, in a religious school play, on a Jewish holiday.

The Hit of the Show!

ON THE WAY HOME DAVID COM-
plained to Debra.

"I'm worried, Debra, you know G'dee. He'll ruin the
play, and that wouldn't be fair to the class."

"Haven't you any faith in your own goat? I have, and
besides I'll spoil G'dee's appetite for at least a half-hour
while the play is going on," Debra was a little frightened.
But she didn't let David see her fear.

When they walked into the house they heard a wild
commotion in the kitchen. In the kitchen they saw G'dee
whirling around in a circle like a pinwheel with a firecracker
in its middle. Shalom was perched on G'dee's right horn
holding on for dear life. Fierce bleats were pouring from
G'dee's throat as he tried to shake the parakeet. Shalom was
having a gay time on his new merry-go-round, refusing to
be budged from his horny perch. When G'dee stopped for
the tiniest minute, Shalom promptly nipped him on the nose
with his sharp beak. With a howling bleat of pain G'dee
began to turn faster and faster like a rocket on its way to
the moon.

86

The twins watched the mad whirl, laughing helplessly until they could laugh no longer. G'dee bleated angrily and Shalom sang merrily. Finally David managed to snatch Shalom and put him into his cage. He closed the cage door on the squawking bird. G'dee crawled under the table exhausted and ashamed over the spectacle he had created over a tiny parakeet. He hid his panting face under his paws.

"I've got it. I've solved our problem, and Shalom is going to help us do it," said Debra.

"What are you talking about?" asked David.

"We can train Shalom to sit on G'dee's horns, and everytime G'dee tries to eat a tree, Shalom can knock it out of his mouth."

"Impossible!" David shook his head as if his sister had suddenly gone mad.

"Let's try," insisted Debra, with a determined shake of her head.

"G'dee won't like it. You know how unhappy he is when Shalom flies near him."

"We can do it, David. I know we can. Somehow or

other we must make G'dee and Shalom become friends." She bent down under the table and patted G'dee, blowing him a butterfly kiss.

G'dee crept out from under the table, and nuzzled his head into Debra, and then into David. Both children gave him a hug, and he felt a little better right away. He glared at Shalom in his cage, but Shalom was too busy kissing himself in the mirror. "Conceited," bleated G'dee, "you certainly love yourself."

Yes, the parakeet and the goat had to become friends. The problem was *how?*

This called for a family conference. Daddy and Mother and David and Debra sat down together and decided on a way to attack the problem. They all agreed that Shalom should be taught to say "G'dee" first. In a short time Shalom was saying "G'dee" clearly. Then, while Debra patted G'dee on the back lovingly, David put Shalom on G'dee's horn.

"G'dee," said David, shaking his finger at the parakeet.

"G'dee," chirped Shalom. He tried to nip G'dee on the nose, but David said, "No, Shalom," and gave him a light spank on his tail feathers.

They did this again and again. At first G'dee tried to shake the parakeet off but after a while, whenever he heard Shalom say "G'dee," he was pleased. He stood quietly with Shalom resting on his horn. After all, this was a game, and he was an important part of the new game. Besides, he wasn't lonely any more. The twins were giving him their undivided attention.

Now they had to train Shalom to knock the tree out of G'dee's mouth. First David put a small tree between his lips. Debra brought Shalom close to David's mouth. It worked! Shalom snatched the tree away, and flew to the kitchen sink with it. There he dropped it with an excited chirp. Then Debra tried it—and Mother—and Daddy—and now came the hard part. What would G'dee do when they put the tree into his mouth? Would he gobble it up before the parakeet could grab it?

A surprise was in store for the Manns. G'dee actually allowed—he really and truly allowed Shalom to take the tree out of his mouth without any objection whatsoever. If the whole family was doing it, he could see no good reason to be stubborn. He knew how to cooperate!

The twins harnessed a small cart to G'dee, and he pulled it across the living-room. Shalom was on G'dee's horn trilling a gay tune. Debra placed a tree in G'dee's mouth, and Shalom snatched it out as quick as a flash. The parakeet dropped it into the cart and jumped on it. G'dee looked at them as if they had all lost their minds, but as long as they were including him in all this nonsense, he didn't care, no, not one bit.

The play began at eleven o'clock. The auditorium was darkened, and the footlights flooded the stage with a rosy light. The piano played a march, and the rear doors opened wide. Down the aisles on both sides came the children of the third grade, each child carrying a small tree, marching in time to the music. They sang *Atzai Zaisim Omdim*, "The Olive Trees Are Standing." Up onto both sides of the stage they walked. They placed their trees against a huge tree stump in the center, and stood in a semi-circle on the stage.

A back curtain parted and Debra, the Queen of the Trees, appeared dressed in a white robe. On her head was a white crown with white paper branches attached to it. She looked as if a tree was growing out of her head. She mounted the tree stump. "I am the Queen of the Trees," she said, looking out into the darkened auditorium. "Thank you, little children for the saplings you have brought. Come let us celebrate the holiday of Tu Bi-Sh'vot, the joyous New Year of the Trees. In the State of Israel from November to

February it rains a great deal. Mother Nature is fast asleep. All the trees are bare except the olive and the cypress and the pine. The fields are newly ploughed and the tiny seeds are waiting to send their little shoots into the bright, wide world around them."

Debra paused to look at all the children on the stage. Her heart raced wildly.

"When the month of Sh'vot arrives Mother Nature begins to dress herself for spring. Blood red poppies pop up in every field. On the slopes rosy cyclamen nod their dainty heads. The almond tree sends out pretty pink and white blossoms. The birds come back to sing their songs up and down the land. Mother Nature has awakened from her deep slumber, and spring has come once more to the tiny land of Israel."

Debra remained standing on the stump. Everyone on the stage sang a song.

> Oh, Tu Bi-Sh'vot has come at last
> In Israel, now the winter's past.
>
> Spring has come, its fragrance bringing,
> Trees are growing, birds are singing,
>
> I'll take my spade to dig and dig,
> I'll plant a tree to grow so big,
>
> On Tu Bi-Sh'vot we'll be so gay,
> We'll honor the trees on their holiday.

In sauntered G'dee, dragging an empty cart behind him, with Shalom on his horn. The audience shrieked with laughing delight. David bent down to put the trees around the stump into the cart, but not before G'dee had picked up one of the trees with his mouth. Shalom was ready! He flew off his perch and snatched the tree out of G'dee's mouth, leaving G'dee with a mouth wide open, full of nothing. But instead of dropping the tree into the cart, Shalom flew up with it

to Debra's tree crown, and perched on the very top branch.
Poor little parakeet! How was he to know that Debra's tree
crown was made of paper? Shalom fell on Debra's hair, and
the tree in Shalom's beak fell into G'dee's open mouth, to be
promptly gobbled up in one greedy gulp. Shalom, now
thoroughly frightened, banked his wings, and soared out into
the audience, chirping an excited song.

Debra turned into a statue with eyes like moons. David
was a stone on the stage. The children in the play stood open-
mouthed in amazement. G'dee helped himself to a few more

trees. This accident was an unexpected piece of luck, and he was taking advantage of his good fortune. Miss Baron stood in the wings, wringing her hands in dismay. How was all this going to end?

Shalom flew about in the auditorium and finally landed on the bald head of one of the fathers in the audience. The house lights went up. Shalom stayed on his new perch, happy once more to be on something solid. His song was high and shrill. In between the high notes could be heard, "G'dee, G'dee."

The audience loved it. They roared with laughter, and the bald father laughed loudest of all.

Since it was David's turn to tell how Tu Bi-Sh'vot is celebrated in Israel, he stepped forward and started to speak in a very loud voice. As soon as G'dee heard him, he turned the cart around and dragged it over to stand beside his master. He looked up at David and winked at him. When Shalom saw who was talking, up he flew, straight as a homing pigeon, to perch on David's head. David didn't mind this at all, he was used to practicing his speech with Shalom on his head.

David's voice rang out loud and clear.

"In every village, and in every town, and in every city in the State of Israel, the children honor the trees on Tu Bi-Sh'vot. Schools are closed on this gay holiday. The children gather together in front of their schools wearing wreaths of gay flowers. Each child is given a tiny seedling to plant in the forest nearby. As they march along the road to the hills they sing happy songs in praise of the trees that they love. The trees seem to bend their leafy branches in fond greeting as the marchers pass. In the forest the children plant their trees carefully with the help of a grown-up who is an expert tree planter." David looked down at G'dee for encouragement. G'dee was ready as usual. He nuzzled into

David's legs with a happy bleat. David continued, stroking G'dee's head lovingly.

> Dig a hole
> Deep and wide,
> Plant a tree,
> Roots inside.
>
> Shine, O sun,
> Shine all year long.
> Grow, O tree,
> Grow tall and strong.
>
> O dear God,
> Please hear my prayer,
> Bless my tree
> With loving care.

At the end all the children gathered in a happy circle around G'dee and his cart, and danced the Hora.

The curtain closed after that. Then the curtains opened and everyone took a bow. Shalom flew over to sit on G'dee's horn. G'dee stepped forward and gave his best goat bow. The audience roared in its delight. Amid the loud applause you could hear G'dee's bleat and Shalom's song. They knew that they had been the hit of the show for Tu Bi-Sh'vot.

Debra's Purim Idea

IT WAS THE SUNDAY BEFORE PURIM. The children in Miss Baron's class were busy making Purim masks. They were bent over their masks absorbed. It was very quiet in the room. Miss Baron walked around the room chuckling.

Debra was making Queen Esther with long black hair. Rosy hearts hung from Queen Esther's ears, and her mouth was a rosy heart, too.

David's tongue was sticking out of the side of his mouth as he bent over his Haman mask. Out of Haman's head stretched three fat firecrackers. From each ear dangled a smooth slimy snake, coiled and ready to strike. A black mustache twirled and swirled and curled above Haman's mouth. The green face was spotted with round red dots. Haman had a bad case of the chicken-pox.

Debra glanced over at David's mask. "Ugh! How horrible!" she squealed, "I'd hate to meet your Haman on a dark night."

"He was mighty tough. He'd scare me in the dark, too." David added another snake to Haman's necktie.

"Time is up!" said Miss Baron, "hold your masks under your chins, children. Let's look at each other's." The children held up their masks.

94

"They're wonderful—such originality—I'm glad I don't have to vote. I wouldn't know which one to choose."

Nancy's Queen Vashti had a purple chin, a carrot nose, and blue straggly hair tied with a pink ribbon. She looked like a witch. Barbara's King Ahasuerus had red circles on his forehead and blue triangles on his chin. A great tea kettle flattened his head. There were dark smudges under his eyes, as if the king hadn't slept for a week. Robert's Mordecai had a pink beard, a frying pan for a hat, and red flower-pot eyes. Linda's Queen Esther had rainbow colored curls, black cats for eyes, and a pumpkin growing out of her chin.

Most of the boys had made Haman masks. There were bony Haman skeletons, silly Haman clowns, and Wild West Haman villains. One Haman was a space man with purple antennae sticking out of his head. There was a wild Haman from the jungles of Borneo, and an Indian chief Haman with war paint all over his face.

"A very unpopular man, this Haman," said Miss Baron. "And now," Miss Baron raised her hand for silence, "and now—I have an announcement of great importance to make —guaranteed to delight." Miss Baron paused to look at the eager faces in front of her. She said nothing more for a few seconds. Her merry eyes sparkled. Miss Baron liked to tease sometimes.

"Tell us quickly, or I'll burst!" exploded Jonathan, almost falling into the aisle.

Miss Baron grinned. "Next Sunday—at eleven o'clock —in the social hall—in honor of the jolly holiday of Purim— we are going to have a—a—*Purim Carnival!*"

The noise was louder than four waterfalls.

"Yippee!" shouted the class, stamping their feet and clapping their hands.

Miss Baron continued. "And—there are going to be games and prizes and refreshments. Admission to the carnival will be ten cents. The money that we collect is going to the United Jewish Fund and will be given to all our Jewish organizations. This money will be your Shalach Monos for this year. One of the nicest customs we have at Purim time is helping the poor and needy people who need help."

Debra raised her hand. There was a thoughtful expression on her shining face. You could tell that an idea had just been born in her active brain.

"Yes, Debra," nodded Miss Baron.

"I've been thinking. I know how we can make some extra Shalach Monos money for the United Jewish Fund."

"We certainly could use the extra money," said Miss Baron.

David nudged Debra knowingly. He was beginning to catch a glimmer of what was going on in his sister's brain. He was sure that the little white goat would be involved in her plan in some way. He waited.

"G'dee will help. And Miss Baron, you know how G'dee loves to help," the words tumbled out of Debra's mouth in a rush.

Miss Baron was silent. She thought of the Tu Bi-Sh'vot play. She remembered the mischief that seemed to tag after G'dee everywhere he chanced to roam. Before she could say a word, Debra began again. "We could harness G'dee to David's cart, and G'dee could ride around the social hall with somebody in the cart for five cents a ride. We'll make hundreds of nickels that way." Debra ended her speech with a rosy blush and sat down quickly.

The children sat breathlessly on the edges of their seats waiting for Miss Baron's decision.

"We could call the cart King Ahasuerus' Chariot," said David, very pleased with his sister's idea.

Miss Baron looked at Debra's anxious face. She looked at David's anxious face. She looked at the anxious faces of the eager children.

"Purim is a jolly holiday. I think that G'dee can be trusted to give the children a ride in King Ahasuerus' chariot. The children will adore the ride. And—we'll make extra charity money—but—I'll have to ask Mr. Samuel's permission, first," replied Miss Baron with a merry Purim smile.

"Hurrah!" shouted the children, jumping up and down like jack-in-the-boxes that had sprung their springs.

The door opened, and Mr. Samuel came in with some new books for the children's library. Miss Baron was embarrassed because the room was so noisy. The principal looked at her with a knowing smile. "I can see that big things are happening here," he said.

"Miss Baron, ask Mr. Samuel now, please Miss Baron," begged Debra, her cheeks burning with eagerness.

"Ask me what?" Mr. Samuel ruffled Debra's hair.

Miss Baron asked.

Mr. Samuel winked at Miss Baron. "Why that's a wonderful way to celebrate Purim. G'dee is just the goat to help us have a bang-up Purim carnival. Bring G'dee next Sunday morning."

The bell could not be heard above the deafening cheers that rose from the class.

King
Ahasuerus'
Chariot

ON THE MORNING OF PURIM, DEBRA'S
eyes opened at six o'clock.

"Rise and shine!" chirped a brown sparrow, as it
hopped about outside Debra's window-sill.

"Rise and shine!" beamed the sun as it cast its golden
rays on Debra's pillow.

"Rise and shine!" sang Shalom from his cage in the
kitchen.

"Rise and shine!" bleated G'dee, tickling Debra's toes
with his nose under her blanket.

With a gay bubble of laughter Debra leaped out of bed
and scampered into David's room. G'dee bobbed along at
her heels.

> Get up! Get up! You sleepy head,
> Purim's here, and you're still in bed!

Debra sang her poem as she danced around and around
David's bed.

G'dee jumped into David's bed and nipped his ear.
David blinked one eye and then the other. "Purim! At last!"
he crowed.

98

They ran into their parents' bedroom to wake them. Daddy and Mother blinked sleepy eyes at them. "Have a heart, twins," grumbled Daddy, "it's only six o'clock in the morning." Daddy looked at the alarm clock.

G'dee climbed into Daddy's bed and licked his face. Daddy had no choice. He gave up with his hands in the air. "Nice bed. Good-bye bed," he said, patting his pillow with a sigh. Mother chased G'dee off the bed with a hairbrush.

First David painted a sign that read: THE THRILL OF A LIFETIME! TAKE A SENSATIONAL RIDE IN KING AHASUERUS' CHARIOT! ONLY FIVE CENTS! He planned to hang it on the wall of the social hall where G'dee was to be stationed. Debra attached two comical Haman masks to G'dee's horns. He looked like a Purim elf.

"I'll bring G'dee and the cart to religious school before eleven o'clock," promised Daddy. "I'll teach him how to ride his passengers safely around the hall. You'd better let me help quite a bit. That way you'll be able to play some of the carnival games too."

At nine-thirty the twins flew off to religious school. On the bulletin was a surprise for them. On a sign in colored letters they read:

EXTRA CARNIVAL ATTRACTION G'DEE

Under the printing was a picture of a little white goat harnessed to a cart, and on it was printed: KING AHASUERUS' CHARIOT.

The children were clustered about the poster. When they saw the twins, they begged them to tell what G'dee was going to do at the carnival.

"Wait and see!" said the twins in mysterious voices.

First they went to the auditorium. As they came into the door, each child was given a gragger by a P.T.A. mother. The racket they made with the noisemakers sounded like an invasion from Mars. When everyone was seated, Mr. Samuel came out on the stage and put up his hands for silence.

"I'm going to ask you to keep the graggers quiet, now. Everyone will have a chance to use them afterwards to his heart's content."

The lights dimmed in the auditorium. Only the footlights were lit.

"On Thursday night, when it was Purim, the rabbi read the Megillah for you at the services," Mr. Samuel went on. "On the stage, the children of the fifth grade today are going to pantomime the Book of Esther as it is written in the Megillah. On the right side of the stage you will see the

100

Megillah readers. On the left side you will see the characters in the Megillah. They will pantomime the action, as the story unfolds in the Book of Esther. Now! Listen carefully, children, because you are in the play, too." The audience sat up. This was a real surprise.

"Every time you hear the name of Haman just as when we read the Megillah at the services, twirl your graggers with all your might!" He paused to take a deep breath. "Haman!" he shouted.

The children twirled their graggers with all their strength. Around and around went the graggers. The noise was deafening.

The Purim pantomime began.

David and Debra watched with shining eyes. They saw King Ahasuerus banish Queen Vashti from the palace for refusing to come to his banquet. He gave her a shove that sent her flying flat on her face. They heard her say to the king, "Did you have to push me *that* hard?"

"That's what you get for refusing to obey me," snarled the king out of the side of his mouth.

The audience hooted. The Megillah readers continued reading their scrolls. The king couldn't make up his mind which maiden to choose as his new queen. As each girl appeared before him, he made a funny face, and shook his head with a firm "no." Once he shook his head so hard that his golden crown slipped down over his eyes. He kept kicking his long purple robe out of his way. Every time he kicked you could see his long trousers.

When Esther curtsied before him, he whistled a long drawn-out whistle and rolled his eyes. The audience loved King Ahasuerus.

"He's as good as any comedy act on television," said David, his sides aching from laughing.

But best of all, the twins liked the horse that Mordecai

rode through the streets of Shushan. The horse was made up of two boys covered with a white sheet, crawling on their hands and knees. On the front boy·was a white papier-mâché horse's head. Long white crepe paper streamers made a flowing tail. Mordecai was sitting on the front boy, giving the horse a crazy lopsided appearance. Haman led the horse with a thick rope. He kept twirling his fierce black mustache, stalking about the stage, glowering and lowering at the horse and at Mordecai, and at the audience. Around and around spun the graggers.

When Queen Esther told the king about Haman's evil plan to kill all the Jews she pointed her finger at him scornfully. King Ahasuerus sent Haman to the gallows with daggers in his eyes. Haman fell on his knees, and begged the king for mercy. His black mustache fell off, and the king kicked it all over the stage. The king's courtier dragged poor Haman off the stage holding on to his ear.

The graggers raced around and the curtain closed.

Queen Esther parted the closed curtain and came out again. She waited until the children calmed down.

> Up and down the country
> The joyful news spread round.
> Prayers had been answered
> And Jewish freedom found.
>
> Sounds of merry laughter
> In Jewish hearts once more.
> Sounds of gladsome singing
> From every Jewish door.
>
> And so their sorrow turned to joy.
> The Jews of all the nation
> Proclaimed the fourteenth of Ador
> A day of celebration.
>
> And from that ancient day to this,
> Now every single one
> Enjoys the feast of Purim so,
> With laughter and with fun.

The Purim pantomime was over. Now came the carnival. The children trooped down to the social hall.

David and Debra didn't know where to look first. Around the walls small booths were set up with gaily painted signs announcing the Purim games. Each booth was manned by a different father. The fathers were standing behind their booths shouting their wares. It sounded like the side show in the circus.

Debra loved the animal balloons floating from the poles. There were low-slung dachshunds and cats with high arched backs. Near them were masks with mysterious cellophane eyes. On the window-sills were clever Purim puppets of all the characters in the Megillah. Purim magic was spread over everything and everybody.

On the stage stood Mr. Rosen, the manager of the carnival. All about him were heaped huge boxes overflowing with prizes. Mr. Rosen was standing in front of a microphone. His voice boomed into it. "Redeem your tickets here! We have prizes for all of you! Play a game and win a prize! Win a prize!"

His voice reached out to every corner of the hall.

G'dee had a corner all to himself. He stood patiently in front of his cart-chariot waiting for his first rider. Mr. Mann stood beside him. In his hand was a megaphone. He put the megaphone to his lips.

"Come and get a ride. Only five cents. All the money goes to charity," he called, smiling down at the masks on G'dee's horns. Soon there was a line of eager children waiting for a turn around the social hall.

Daddy had drawn a thick white chalk line in a circle for the route, and G'dee had practiced again and again. He knew exactly how to keep on the line with the cart. Into the cart went the first little boy. Around the white circle tripped G'dee carrying his precious cargo. End of ride number one! Into the chariot went another boy, and a girl, and a boy, and another girl. Soon Mr. Mann's pocket was heavy with nickels. Business was booming! The line never shortened. Some of the children wanted two rides, but Daddy had to refuse.

"When everybody has had one chance, I'll begin on the second round," he promised.

G'dee felt so helpful. He trotted around proudly, his pointed head in the air, his snub-nosed tail wagging gaily from side to side. Many of the children were feeding him candy. "Feed me! Feed me!" he bleated, "this is hard work, and I need plenty of energy."

The twins were busy playing Purim games.

David heaved a ball down King Ahasuerus' bowling alley. Down went five pins. A red ticket slipped into his hand. David grinned.

Debra spun the wheel on Queen Esther's menagerie. It stopped on the lion, the animal she had chosen before she spun the wheel. A red ticket slipped into her eager hand. Debra grinned.

David tossed a rubber ring on Haman's long finger. Another red ticket! David's eyes sparkled.

Debra threw a bean bag into Haman's open mouth. Into the hole it fell with a loud plop. Another red ticket! Debra's eyes sparkled.

The twins now had two tickets apiece. They ran to the stage and gave the tickets to Mr. Rosen. Into Debra's hands dropped a long string of rainbow colored beads. Debra

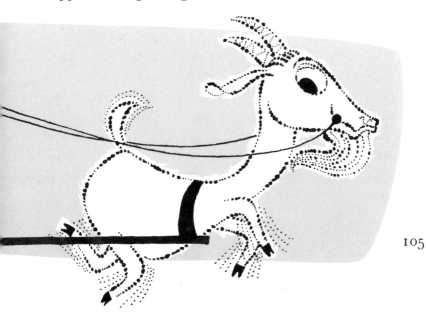

draped them around her neck. Into David's hands went a white rubbery skeleton. He dangled it in front of Debra. She squealed in make-believe fright.

Back to the booths they scrambled to try their luck again.

David shot some golf at the Shushan golf course. With a toy club he putted a small white ball straight into the hole on the miniature green.

"A hole in one!" said the father in charge of the booth. "For that skilful putt you get two tickets." David beamed like the sun.

Debra hooked a rubber ring on Haman's turned-up nose. She missed the next ring, but on the third try she hooked Haman's nose again. Her eyes were stars as she got the two red tickets.

David shot some darts in the Shushan shooting gallery. *A bull's-eye!* Into his outstretched hand went another ticket. David's left dimple danced.

Debra shot a cork from a toy gun at Esther's Royal Owls. Down went an owl with red staring eyes. Plop! Plop! Plop! Down fell three more owly owls.

"Three tickets to the best shot in Brookline," called the father. Debra's right dimple danced.

The twins ran to Mr. Rosen again to redeem their tickets. He chuckled, "This is your lucky day, isn't it?"

"You bet!" said David, choosing a striped green turtle. Mr. Rosen showed him how to wind it. David put it on the floor and the turtle jumped off the stage. Debra chose a colorful fan with a picture of Queen Esther on it. "Let's watch G'dee, now, so that Daddy can have a rest," she said.

"Right-o," agreed David.

G'dee was coming back with a laughing passenger.

When he saw the twins he winked at them. He had forgotten them completely. Business had been so rushed.

"Daddy, why don't you take a rest for awhile. We'll watch G'dee," said Debra, making eyes at Daddy from behind her fan.

"I think that I'll do just that." Daddy was longing for a cigarette. "But be careful. We don't want any accidents."

The twins promised to be careful and took over. David announced the rides like his father, through the megaphone.

Alex was next to hop into the chariot. G'dee trotted off around the circle. Suddenly one of the corks shot into his face from a gun aimed the wrong way. G'dee leaped into the air. He veered off the white line, and headed for the race track booth. Down went the booth on a father. G'dee galloped through the golf course booth butting another father, and tossing him against the wall. He flew through the booths in great long leaps knocking them down like bowling pins. G'dee was forked lightning. Poor Alex! Up into the air he went, high, high like a flying bird. Mr. Samuel ran over to where he guessed Alex would fall, and stretched his arms out. *Thump!* Into his waiting arms fell Alex, almost flattening Mr. Samuel like a pancake.

David and Debra collapsed with laughter. The children had stopped their games to watch the fun. A roar punctured the air of the social hall. Suddenly G'dee stopped dead in his tracks, and squatted down on the floor. He was exhausted. He gazed at the shambles he had caused, and nodded his head sadly. "I always manage to get into trouble," he bleated in a whimper, "I was really trying so hard! I was doing my Purim best."

But the fathers and the children weren't angry with G'dee at all. Everyone had had a rip-roaring laugh. This was jolly Purim, and who wants to be cross at Purim time?

Alex ran over to G'dee who immediately drooped his pointed head in shame. Alex grinned and patted G'dee on the back. "Don't feel so sad, G'dee. I had a wonderful time up there in the air. Now I know how it feels to be an airplane." G'dee wagged his tail. He felt much better now.

The fathers set up the booths in their proper places again. The games went on as before. Most of the children crowded around G'dee.

Mr. Rosen boomed into the megaphone. "Here they come! The mothers' parade!" Into the social hall came the mothers of the P.T.A., carrying heaping trays of crisp, brown cakes shaped like triangles filled with poppy seeds.

"Homontaschen!" drooled the children with hungry eyes. "Homontaschen!" drooled the fathers with hungry, hungry eyes. "Homontaschen!" bleated G'dee, forgetting his troubles as his eyes lingered on the crunchy cakes.

The trays emptied quickly. Again and again all the Mothers ran back to the kitchen for more homontaschen. G'dee had four because he was the star performer of the carnival.

Mr. Rosen called for attention through his megaphone. "Did everyone have a good time?"

"Yes!" shouted the children.

108

"Did all the fathers have a good time?"

"Yes!" shouted the fathers, making believe that their knees were buckling under them.

"Three cheers for G'dee," called Mr. Rosen.

"G'dee! G'dee! G'dee!" rang the voices of the children.

G'dee crossed his legs in a beautiful goat bow. One of the masks slipped off his horns, and caught onto his beard but he didn't mind that at all. Those homontaschen kept him busy.

Debra sang a Purim poem all the way home.

> Here comes Purim,
> Dance and sing,
> Happy voices
> Gaily ring.
>
> Hear the Megillah,
> The story that's old.
> Thrill to brave Esther
> And Mordecai bold.
>
> Come twirl your graggers
> Round and round.
> Eat homontaschen
> By the pound.
>
> Shalach Monos
> Gifts bestow,
> Loving thoughts
> To those we know.
>
> Let's give Purim
> A rousing good cheer,
> Gayest, merriest
> Time of the year.

Out, Chomets!

ON THE DAY BEFORE PASSOVER, Daddy and David liked to search the house for chomets. G'dee searched for chomets. Shalom, perched on G'dee's horns, searched for chomets too.

David carried the dust pan and brush with which to scoop up the unwelcome chomets. They trooped into the living-room.

"Fee-fie-fo-fum, here I come, little crumb," sang David, looking under the piano.

Pounce! David spied a piece of bread. He whisked it into the dust pan. G'dee lunged for the crumb, but Shalom was quicksilver. He swooped down from G'dee's horn and gobbled up the crumb in a flash.

Daddy spotted a cake crumb near the fireplace. "Come and get it, David!"

Whisk! Into the dust pan went the cake. Again G'dee tried to snatch it and again Shalom was lightning. G'dee glared at his greedy little friend. That Shalom was getting his goat. G'dee tried to shake Shalom from his horn, but the little parakeet clung to his favorite perch, singing merrily.

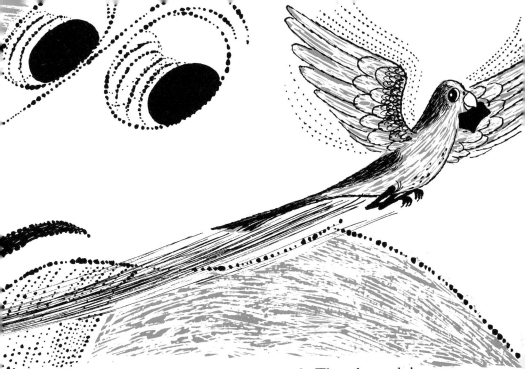

Into the dining-room they tramped. They hunted in
every corner. "I've found one," shouted David from under
the table. He crawled out holding a piece of biscuit. G'dee
looked at David hungrily, begging for the biscuit with his
eyes. Shalom flew onto David's head waiting to be fed.

"It's G'dee's turn, Shalom," and David popped the
cracker into G'dee's mouth.

"Traitor!" squawked Shalom, nipping David's ear.

Into the kitchen they strolled single file. Here they
stopped short. The Passover fragrance of cooking drifted
into their nostrils making their mouths water. On top of
the kitchen range something was bubbling merrily in a
gleaming copper pot. Through the glass oven door they
could see a Passover sponge cake rising high as a golden
tower.

G'dee edged slowly over to the range, but David pulled
him back by the tail. Shalom flew off G'dee's horn and
perched his dainty feet near a fresh jelly roll on the table.
His inquisitive little beak plunged deep down into the jelly
roll. The beak came out smeared with gobs of bright rasp-

berry jelly. Over to G'dee's mouth flew the parakeet. Into G'dee's surprised mouth dipped the jellied beak.

"That's more like it," bleated G'dee, licking the jelly off Shalom's beak.

"This is already a Passover kitchen. No crumbs of chomets here," said Daddy. "Let's search in the bedrooms now."

But this time Daddy and David left alone. The goat and the parakeet wouldn't budge. The kitchen was too pleasant a place to leave. There was *food* here—not eensy, teensy, weensy, crumby, crumbs, no bigger than flies.

A moment later Daddy and David returned.

"Who wants to ride over to Coolidge Corner with me to buy some Passover flowers?" asked Daddy.

"I do!" shouted the twins at the same time.

G'dee didn't move. He was glued to the kitchen with the food. Mother and Grandmother had a very kind way of giving him the left-overs.

Shalom stayed with G'dee. The kitchen was an interesting place for parakeets too. And besides G'dee owed him something for that jelly he had given him before.

Up the shining length of Beacon Street Father and children whizzed to the florist. Daddy let Debra choose the flowers. She chose sunny jonquils, tall red gladioli, long-stemmed roses, and glossy huckleberry leaves. Daddy added some larkspur because they reminded him of Debra's blue eyes. They laid the lovely flowers in the back of the car and rode home singing merrily.

When they came home they found the house shiny and clean. Every room in the house sparkled with fresh spring radiance. The happy spirit of Passover hovered over everything and everybody. Grandmother and Mother were in the living-room, resting their weary feet after the hard day's work. G'dee was sprawled on the floor chewing Mother's shoe. Shalom was perched on Grandmother's head, trying to pull strands of silver hair from under her hair net.

"Debra, take that bird off my hair or I'll be bald for the Passover Seder," laughed Grandmother, shaking her head. Debra snatched Shalom and spanked him lightly on his tail feathers.

"And now it's time to give G'dee his Passover bath," announced Daddy, rolling up his sleeves.

"I'll help," said David with a grin.

"Me, too," said Debra, "as soon as I help Mother finish arranging the flowers."

G'dee rolled over with a bounce. "Oh, no, you don't," he bleated, bounding out of the room to hide. He wasn't having any old bath even if it was a holiday. The soap had a way of dripping into his ears and eyes and nose. The water was too wet, and he had no appetite for soap even if it *did* smell good.

But G'dee was outnumbered. They cornered him just as he was trying to sneak into the pantry. Daddy hauled the struggling, bleating goat into the bathroom. The twins followed and closed the door.

Mother and Grandmother clapped their hands over their ears. The moans and groans coming from behind the closed door could be heard in Timbuctoo. The splashing and the gurgling told them that their shiny white bathroom was no longer clean for Passover, but G'dee was!

He was sparkling white from the tip of his button nose to the end of his snubby tail. He lay down on the rug. It had been a fierce struggle.

Daddy came out as wet as the Atlantic Ocean.

Debra came out as wet as the Pacific Ocean.

David came out as wet as the Indian Ocean.

Mother went into the bathroom to mop up the flood.

The Mann ranch house was ready for Passover.

I'm a Free Goat, Too

G'DEE STOOD AT THE TOP OF THE stairs leading to the playroom. He pawed at the closed door and butted with lowered horns. "David! Debra! How can you do this to me on the first night of Passover? Let me out!" he bleated.

Upstairs the family was getting ready to sit down to the Passover Seder. The twins faced Daddy with faces long as telephone poles.

"Daddy, please let G'dee come to the Passover Seder. He's never seen one before," begged Debra.

"Now, look here, Debra, we don't want anything to disturb the Seder tonight. Let's have a little peace for a change." Daddy's voice was firm. "G'dee won't behave, and you know it!"

G'dee scratched at the door again and bleated mournfully. Debra put her hands to her ears, wincing at the pleading in G'dee's voice.

David turned to Grandfather for help. "Grandpop, why do we celebrate Passover?"

Grandfather looked at David in surprise. "God guided

Moses as he led the Children of Israel out of slavery in Egypt to freedom. Passover marks the beginning of the Jewish people as a free nation." Grandfather looked at David's eager face. "But you know that, David," he added, a puzzled look on his face.

"Well, then, if we're celebrating the freedom that came to us at Passover time, why does G'dee have to be jailed in the playroom? He'd like to be free, too."

Grandfather's eyes smiled at David. He was beginning to understand David's argument. He looked at Debra but she was silent.

"Please let Daddy change his mind," she wished inside herself.

Grandfather turned to Daddy. "What do you say, son? Do we make G'dee a free goat for Passover?"

Daddy looked at Mother and Grandmother. They nodded their heads in agreement. Daddy gave up and moved to the playroom door. He opened it and sidestepped quickly as G'dee swept through the door like a jet-propelled engine.

G'dee ran from one member of the family to another, switching his tail back and forth. "I'm a free goat," he bleated, his face glowing with new-found freedom, "and I want to celebrate *my* freedom at the Seder."

The twins bent down to pat him tenderly. "Please be a good goat tonight, G'dee," begged Debra. David dragged a chair to the right corner of the table next to Grandfather. With a nimble leap G'dee scrambled onto the chair. He sat on his haunches and smiled a beautiful goat smile.

"Now that I'm here, what are we waiting for? Let's begin now—this very second," he ma-a-a-ed, gazing with interest at the Passover table.

Everyone sat down. G'dee looked with love at each one in his family. He smiled at Grandfather at the head of the table, sitting in an armchair with a pillow under his arm. He smiled at Daddy seated at Grandfather's right hand. He smiled at David at Grandfather's left hand. He winked at Debra next to David, and he winked at Mother next to Daddy, and he double winked at Grandmother seated opposite Grandfather at the foot of the table. My, but he loved them—each and every one of them.

G'dee looked at the table again. He smacked his lips at the shining crystal goblets filled with wine. But there were many special things on the table tonight, things that he had never seen before in all his goat life. His gaze lingered on a copper plate divided into sections. Each groove had something different in it. He saw a lamb bone, a roasted egg, horseradish, fresh green parsley, and charoses. "A pretty strange mixture," he bleated, "but I'd like a sample of everything just the same."

G'dee noticed a tall silver cup next to the Seder plate. It was filled to the top with wine, too. He wondered about that. Was that the cup that David called Elijah's cup? He guessed it was. He could see no other reason why it should be standing in the middle of the table all by itself.

"Grandpop, you're sitting up too straight. On this night you're supposed to relax," said David with a grin, winking at G'dee.

"Right you are, David, my boy," Grandfather laughed as he leaned against the pillow on his chair. "Tonight I will

116

lean on my pillow in remembrance of the freedom that came to us when we left Egypt."

G'dee leaned back against the back of the chair. "I'm a free goat, too," he ma-a-a-ed at everyone.

The service began. Grandfather chanted the Passover Kiddush, thanking God for this joyous holiday. His eyes shone as he looked around the table at his family. Quietly, to himself, he thanked God for his happiness.

Everyone repeated the prayer for wine. Lifting the tall goblets filled to the brim with sweet wine, each one at the table took a sip. G'dee stared at David's goblet. He saw the goblet in David's hand move slowly toward him. "That's better," bleated G'dee, when the wine came to a halt at his mouth. He ran his tongue around the brim of the goblet, and took a deep sip, and a deeper sip, but David withdrew the wine and placed it on the table.

"No more now, G'dee, there are three more sips to come. You'll get sleepy, and you'll miss the rest of the Seder. This is only the beginning of good things to come, especially for a goat."

G'dee bleated in disappointment. But he watched Grandfather take a piece of parsley from the Seder plate and dip it into some salt water. He said the prayer for vegetables. The parsley passed about the table, and everyone took a sprig, and dipped it into salt water.

"I know why we dip it into salt water," said Debra, chewing the parsley with a wry expression on her face. "The salt water reminds us of the tears our ancestors shed when they were slaves in Egypt. And I don't like it a bit!"

"Give G'dee a piece, Dad," said Father.

Grandfather dipped a piece of parsley into the salt water, and put it into G'dee's already waiting mouth.

G'dee gobbled it up in one gulp. He puckered up his lips, and made a sour face like Debra.

Grandfather held up a folded napkin with three pieces of matso tucked in between the folds.

"These three pieces of matso represent three divisions of the Jewish people, the Kohanim, or priests, the Levites, who served the priests, and the Israelites. I am going to break the middle matso into two unequal parts, and hide it. Whoever finds it," Grandfather paused to wink at the twins, "whoever finds it, will receive a fine gift—a mighty fine gift."

David's right dimple smiled. Debra's left dimple smiled. They loved the presents that their grandparents chose for them.

"David, since you are the youngest boy, it is your turn to ask the *Four Questions* in Hebrew," said Grandfather.

David's voice was as clear as a bell as he chanted the four questions. He was proud to be able to sing the ancient melody seated at his own table surrounded by his own loving family—he knew that Jewish boys all over the world were chanting the four questions using the same tune.

Debra translated the Hebrew into English. G'dee bleated all the time that Debra was talking. He was asking the four questions in his own goat language.

"The answers to your questions, children, can be found in our ancient Haggadah," said Grandfather, holding up a book. "In this book of Passover we are told how God took our forefathers out of Egypt, with Moses, leading them. It tells us how our ancestors were slaves, and how they built great cities for the Pharaoh. It tells us how God freed Israel and brought them to Mount Sinai." Grandfather read on in the Haggadah. Everybody had a turn to read. G'dee wished he could read so he could have a part too.

On and on they read in the Haggadah. Debra and David were beginning to get hungry, but they didn't complain. They tried to be grown-up. G'dee lolled his head to the side. This was taking a long time, but he was determined to be a good goat. He watched everyone carefully.

"What is the meaning of Pesach?" asked Grandmother.

Grandfather held up the roasted bone for everyone to see. "Pesach means the paschal lamb. It was the sacrifice our ancestors made because the Lord passed over the houses of the Children of Israel in Egypt when the plagues came. So may He always protect us from slavery and all other evils."

G'dee looked at the bone. The juicy meat made his mouth water but he knew that the bone was not to be eaten. "I can wait," he bleated at the twins. David and Debra laughed at the expression on their goat's face.

Daddy asked, "What is the meaning of matso?"

Grandfather held up a piece of matso for everyone to see.

"Our ancestors left Egypt in great haste. On their shoulders they carried trays on which they kneaded their bread. Later they baked the bread in the hot desert sun."

G'dee stared at the matso. His mouth watered again at the sight of the crisp, crunchy cracker, but he made no attempt to get it. "This is special matso, and I know it," he bleated, rolling his tongue around his mouth.

Mother said, "What is the meaning of moror?"

Grandfather held up the horseradish. "These are the bitter herbs that stand for the bitter lives our ancestors led when they were slaves in Egypt." He set the plate down right in front of G'dee's nose. The bitter smell of the horse-radish brought tears to his eyes.

"Not for me," he bleated. He pushed the plate away with his paw.

Grandfather said the prayer for wine, and for the second time everyone took a sip of the wine.

"My head is beginning to feel dizzy," giggled Debra, "I'm going around in circles."

"That's because you're hungry, darling," said Mother.

Grandfather gave G'dee a sip of wine. He turned to the twins. "Just a little longer, twins, and we'll be ready to eat."

In that second G'dee guzzled the wine to the very last drop. The wine went directly to his head. He tried to stand up but instead his head rolled to the back of the chair. "That wine is making me sleepy," he bleated, "I must force myself to stay awake. I wouldn't want to miss one minute of this wonderful Seder. No, indeed!"

Grandfather took the upper matso from the plate. Breaking it into pieces he passed it around the table. Everyone said the prayer for matso, and ate a piece. David gave some to G'dee. The matso crackled in G'dee's mouth. A crumb slipped out onto the carpet. G'dee eyed the crumb but didn't stir. "I'll get you later when I'm wide awake again," he bleated at the crumb.

"Now comes the time for everyone to make a Hillel

sandwich," announced Grandfather. He spread some horse-radish and charoses between two pieces of the upper matso, and said the prayer for moror.

Debra said, "I remember why. The bitter herbs stand for the bitterness of our slavery in Egypt."

David added, "The charoses reminds us of the bricks the children of Israel made when they were building cities for the Pharaohs."

Grandfather nodded proudly at the twins. "Our people never lost courage. They always held on to the hope that their slavery would end."

"Mother, the charoses is yummy. I can taste the nuts and the wine and the apples and the cinnamon. It hides the bitterness of the horseradish," said Debra.

David laughed. "No wonder you can taste the charoses. I saw you make that sandwich. You piled on the charoses and used just a little horseradish."

Debra made a face at her brother. "I love charoses, and I don't like horseradish at all. So there!"

Grandfather made a sandwich for G'dee who was lean-ing sleepily against the back of the chair. The tangy sand-wich revived him somewhat.

"Time to eat!" said Grandfather, patting G'dee on the head.

G'dee and the twins perked up and sat up straight in their chairs. Their eyes gleamed with excitement as they watched Mother and Grandmother hustle and bustle out of the dining-room.

What a feast! They loved the hard boiled eggs in salt water. It tasted so good, especially at Passover time. They adored the gefilte fish, and the chicken soup with fluffy matso balls. David waved a turkey drumstick at G'dee trying to attract his attention. But G'dee was too busy eating his *own* turkey and his *own* vegetable stuffing and his *own* cranberries.

For dessert they had sponge cake covered with lemon sauce. Debra was too stuffed to eat her dessert but G'dee was glad to help her out. "You mustn't waste a bit of this scrumptious food, Debra," he bleated, licking the blob of cranberry and the blob of lemon sauce that had rolled down into his beard.

After dinner Grandfather smiled at the twins. "The time has come to find the afikomon, twins. Remember the matso I hid at the beginning of the Seder? We need to find it now because it is our dessert matso."

David and Debra sprang up from the table. Debra looked under Grandfather's pillow, and David searched under the table. They found nothing. Grandfather hinted in a low voice behind his hand, "The window-sill, the window-sill."

With a flying leap G'dee jumped from his chair, and bounded over to the window-sill. But David was quicker. Grabbing the afikomon, he waved it in the air. "I've found it! I've found it!"

G'dee pulled at David, trying to snatch the matso, but Debra caught him on the horn. "Go back to your chair, G'dee. We all have to eat the afikomon. We'll give you a piece too. Just be patient." And wonder of wonders! Back to his seat he trotted. He scrambled onto his chair, sat on his haunches, and scratched his ear with his paw.

Everyone ate a piece of the afikomon, including the little white goat.

Grandmother put a package on the table. In it the twins found a printing set for David, and a toy sewing machine for Debra. G'dee looked at Grandmother. "And me, what do I get?" he ma-a-a-a-ed at her.

Grandmother didn't disappoint G'dee. From a small box she drew a rubber bone. She put it on G'dee's chair. G'dee rubbed his nose against it. "Rubber bone!" he bleated. "Come now, Grandma, after the Passover feast I've just had! Are you trying to be funny?"

They drank the third cup of wine. This time G'dee pushed David's goblet away. He was stuffed to his ears, thank you.

When it was time to open the door for Elijah, David went to the front door. He opened it and his mouth opened in astonishment. Standing in the door was Joseph Adams, their baby sitter, holding a bottle of wine in his hand.

"Come in, Elijah," invited David.

"Come in, who?" asked Joseph, wondering at his new name. "I just walked over to bring you a present for Passover."

"I opened the door for Elijah, and you walked in sporting a sport jacket."

They walked into the dining-room. Joseph gave the wine to Mrs. Mann.

They drank the fourth cup of wine.

"Join us in the singing, Joseph. You can follow the

music in this book and we can use your mighty baritone," said Daddy. And then the singing began. The old Passover songs filled the room with beauty and happiness. G'dee loved "Chad Gadyo" best because it told about a little goat.

Debra and David put their arms about their little white goat.

"This is your song, G'dee," chanted Debra, tweaking G'dee's right ear.

"This is your special song, G'dee," chanted David, tweaking G'dee's left ear. G'dee looked up at the twins, his eyes lighting up with love. "I am a lucky goat to take part in a Passover Seder with such a wonderful family," he bleated.

"Chad Gadyo," sang everyone, their faces beaming.

"Chad Gadyo," chirped Shalom from his cage in the kitchen.

"Chad Gadyo," bleated G'dee, his little goat heart pounding with Passover happiness. "Why," he thought, "I bet that even I could write a poem. Let's see:

> "The search for afikomon
>   Is a job that's just for me,
> To find the crunchy matso
>   A detective I must be.
>
> "Under the Seder table,
>   Under my Daddy's chair,
> Under my grandpop's pillow,
>   Where can it be, oh, where?
>
> "But when at last I spy it,
>   Then my joy is quite complete,
> I burst out loud with laughter
>   And I dance around my seat.
>
> "Finding the afikomon
>   Brings a gift that's just for me,
> Pesach is so delightful,
>   Fills my heart with gaiety."

The Lag Bo-omer Rainbow Goat

DAVID AND DEBRA WERE DOWN-
stairs in the playroom painting eggs for the Lag Bo-omer
picnic. Miss Baron was taking her entire religious school class
to Franklin Park to celebrate the holiday the next day. The
twins' eyes danced with excitement. Three of the mothers
were going, too, to help Miss Baron take care of the children.

Miss Baron had asked the children to bring the refreshments for the picnic. David and Debra had volunteered to
bring the eggs. Mother had boiled the eggs, and now the
twins were painting them. Their work table was littered with
cups of gaily colored paint. David had experimented with
different color blendings, and produced a heavenly shade of
blue, a strawberry pink, a daffodil yellow, a jack-o-lantern
orange, a leafy green, and a lipstick red.

Suddenly Debra had a brainstorm. She painted a leafy
green tree on a strawberry pink egg, and held it up for David
to admire. A beam of dazzling sunlight danced on the egg.

"This is the tree that Bar Kochba pulled up by its roots
as he rode by on his white horse," she said with a chuckle,
"just like Superman."

126

David laughed. "Hey, Debra, that's a dandy idea. Let's paint Lag Bo-omer scenes on all the eggs. The class will get a great kick out of eggs that have a story to tell."

Debra was delighted with her brother's suggestion. She painted a glittering rainbow on a white egg. "This is the rainbow that appeared when the great Rabbi Simeon ben Yochai died on Lag Bo-omer. I'm glad there was a rainbow especially for him. Imagine teaching the Torah in a cave for thirteen years, while hiding from the Romans."

David painted a bonfire on a heavenly blue egg. "This is the bonfire around which the Israeli people dance and sing in Meron on Lag Bo-omer in honor of Simeon ben Yochai who is buried there."

Debra painted a red bow and arrow on a daffodil yellow egg. "This is the bow and arrow that the Jewish boys and girls carried into the woods when they went secretly to study the Torah with Rabbi Akiba."

David painted another leafy tree, this time on a yellow egg. "This is the tree in the woods that hid the Roman soldier who wanted to know where the boys were going," he giggled, placing the egg on the table to dry.

Debra painted a Torah on an orange egg. "This is the Torah that our brave rabbis kept alive in those bad days. If they hadn't kept the Torah alive in the people's hearts we might not be having a Lag Bo-omer picnic tomorrow." David frowned at his sister. "What a horrible thought," he said, shuddering.

"Do you think that the boys were afraid when they met the Roman soldiers in the woods, David?"

"They had to be brave. The rabbis were, and the boys had to follow their example. Anyway, I'm sure that they looked those nosy soldiers straight in the eyes and didn't flicker an eyelash." David's voice was steely.

David finished painting a red sword on a yellow egg. "This is the sword of Bar Kochba who raised the mighty army to fight the Romans."

Debra painted some stones on a red egg, and held it up. David stared. "Stones! What have they to do with Lag Bo-omer?" He was really puzzled this time.

Debra lifted her hands in great surprise. "Don't you remember Miss Baron's story about the Jewish superman; the one about the Roman machines that hurled stones at the Jewish army when they were behind the walls at Bethar? Bar Kochba caught the flying stones and flung the stones right back into their faces with his iron knees."

"What a man! He was a super superman!"

Debra jumped up. Standing with her feet apart she flung her arms in the air.

> Hail to Bar Kochba
> Son of a star,
> Great was his courage
> Famed near and far.
>
> Hail to Bar Kochba
> Hero of old,
> Great was his power
> Superman bold.
>
> Hail to Bar Kochba
> Soldier of fame,
> Fighter for freedom
> May we be the same.

The playroom door opened upstairs and Mother appeared. "Children," she called, "time for lunch!"

"I'm as hungry as a bear!" said Debra, racing up the stairs.

"I'm as hungry as double trouble bears!" said David, following her.

They forgot to close the playroom door. G'dee had been hovering near that door all morning waiting to be admitted. But—because he had a little weakness for paint, the twins had not allowed G'dee to join them in the Lag Bo-omer fun. All because he had licked the newly painted kitchen table before it was dry.

The open door was a golden opportunity for G'dee to find out what he had missed. Down the stairs he scrambled, tumbling over into a somersault in his eagerness to investigate. He came to a sudden halt. His eyes peered at the bright eggs. He sniffed at the fresh paint.

"Paint on eggs!" he bleated joyously, poking at the rainbow egg nearest to the table edge with his nose. Lowering his right horn he crashed the egg on the floor. He peeled

the cracked egg with his lips, and the Lag Bo-omer egg slipped smoothly down his throat.

The same happened to the bow and arrow egg and to the Torah egg. When he came to the tree egg, his eyes gleamed. *"Trees on eggs! Double delicious!"* he bleated, a song in his heart.

He was suddenly thirsty. Looking about the table, he spied the cups of colored water. But he didn't care. Water was water no matter the color! On to the work table he jumped. He lapped up the strawberry paint and the heavenly blue paint. Down his throat trickled the jonquil yellow and the lipstick red and the leafy green and the jack-o-lantern orange water. His pointed head didn't lift until every drop was gone. All the colors dribbled down into his beard blending into a rainbow. G'dee changed into a funny circus goat with a Lag Bo-omer rainbow beard.

The playroom door opened and the twins tripped down the stairs to finish their work. When they saw G'dee they stretched their hands in the air, horrified.

"G'dee, you naughty goat!" cried Debra, shaking an angry finger at him, "you've ruined our Lag Bo-omer eggs for the picnic!"

"What a mess! You look as if you escaped from a circus side show!" scolded David.

G'dee looked at the twins and dropped his head lower and lower until his rainbow beard swept the floor. He trotted

over to Debra and licked her hand begging her to forgive him. Debra turned away, ignoring him. He trotted over to David and tried to lick his hand. David ignored him just like Debra. G'dee bleated and two glistening goat tears streaked down into his beard.

The twins looked at their pet. They saw the tears. They saw the colored beard. Out whooped a whoop of laughter! Really, G'dee was a comical sight. They couldn't possibly remain angry with such a funny circus clown. Now could they?

Mother came down to see what all the noise was about. When she saw the rainbow beard, she laughed until the tears rolled down her cheeks.

"I'll boil some more eggs," she promised, "and I'll help you paint them."

They set to work again. David had to mix some more paint. In a few hours the eggs were packed away in a basket, each one as pretty as a picture. This time G'dee was satisfied to watch, sprawled by the window. He decided not to touch another drop of paint. He'd had his lesson. He wasn't taking any more chances. That picnic was too close and he didn't want to miss it, not for anything in the world. Anyway, he was stuffed. It was always easier for him to be good when he was stuffed.

Later that night the twins tried to scrub the paint off G'dee's beard but the paint stuck. It would not come off no matter how hard they scrubbed.

"I guess G'dee will have to go to the picnic with a painted beard," sighed Debra. "He's going to look mighty funny."

"He'll scare all the animals in the zoo," laughed **Daddy**.

G'dee looked at Daddy and lifted his eyes scornfully. "What do I care," he bleated, "as long as I go to that Lag Bo-omer picnic with the twins."

A Free Ride

THE NEXT DAY WAS JUST RIGHT FOR a picnic. The sun gleamed like a bright golden coin. Round cream-puff clouds floated in the sky. The bus stopped at the Mann ranch house at one o'clock in the afternoon. Into the bus piled the twins with G'dee tagging at their heels. When the children saw G'dee and his rainbow beard, they roared.

"What's so funny?" G'dee bleated, giving them a saucy look.

Miss Baron patted the painted goat and scratched his ear. G'dee purred with delight. Miss Baron knew how to make a goat feel good.

G'dee squatted up front with Bill, the bus driver, watching the road.

"You must be a goat from another planet," said Bill, out of the side of his mouth.

"Get on with your driving. I can't wait to begin this picnic," ma-a-a-a-ed G'dee, ignoring Bill's remarks.

Everyone sang. They sang "Lag Bo-omer" over and over again because it told about going to the woods with bows and arrows. Resting against the back of the bus was a huge archery set.

The bus stopped in the parking area. Through the great granite pillars they marched into the park. They passed a band playing spangled music in the grandstand, but they didn't stop to listen. Past the lion house, past the elephant house, past the red bird house with its fluted pagoda, they ran. G'dee made a dash for every open door, but David held on tightly to his collar. At the great open bird cage G'dee ma-a-a-a-a-ed at the haughty peacock strutting about with its jeweled feathers spread out like a fan. When they crossed the duck pond G'dee bleated at the white swan sailing lazily by. He rushed at the tiny ducks, and bleated when they wagged their stumpy tails at him.

Miss Baron led the way up a steep path into a piney woods. They entered an open clearing surrounded by tall sweet-smelling fir trees on one side. On the other side was a flower garden. Red rosy tulips and jonquils with golden yellow bonnets bobbed in the breeze.

"This is where we stop," said Miss Baron, spreading a huge blanket on the grass. "Put all the packages in the center of the blanket, and we'll eat our refreshments here."

Onto the blanket they piled the sandwiches and the cakes and the popcorn and the potato chips. G'dee nosed over slowly, his tail wagging furiously. David bent down to whisper something into his ear. G'dee turned about and headed for the flowers.

"I'll do as you say, David," he bleated, with one last fond look at the food.

David set the basket on the blanket. When the children saw the Lag Bo-omer eggs they clapped their hands with delight. Miss Baron was so pleased. "Look, each egg tells something about the holiday we are celebrating," she exclaimed. "Twins, do you mind if I use your idea for religious school next year? The children would enjoy painting eggs."

David and Debra tingled with happiness. Bill came up with the archery set and two cases of soda pop. The mothers carried the prizes. The picnic began.

"Before we begin to play games," said Miss Baron, "let's do something in honor of the holiday we are celebrating. Any ideas?"

The children put their fingers to their temples and thought. Judy said, "Let's play Lag Bo-omer charades."

Miss Baron asked, "How many children like Judy's idea?" All the hands went up in the air waving wildly.

The girls formed one team and the boys another. David was chosen to captain the boys, and Debra was chosen to captain the girls. Their Lag Bo-omer eggs convinced the children that the twins had good ideas.

G'dee was busy chasing grasshoppers. He didn't want

to play charades. David and the boys walked away from the group and plotted their charade. They came back with happy smiles. The girls would never guess the brilliant charade they had hatched together.

David ran out in front of the children waving a thick branch. He thrust it up and down in the air. Lunging to one side he plunged the branch into one boy and lunging to the other side he plunged the branch into another boy. Richard walked slowly toward David. He pretended that he was reading a book. Everytime he turned a page, he lifted his eyes and nodded his head sadly.

Richard said, "Guess!" The girls were quiet. Miss Baron didn't say anything. Suddenly Judy jumped up from the grass. "I know! I know! It's easy as pumpkin pie!"

"All right, Judy, what is it?" asked David, who didn't believe Judy knew at all.

"You are Bar Kochba fighting the Romans with your sword, and Richard is Rabbi Akiba reading the Torah. Rabbi Akiba didn't want war, that's why he shook his head sadly at Bar Kochba." Judy ran her words together in her excitement.

Debra interrupted. "But Rabbi Akiba did want Bar Kochba to fight. Didn't he help Bar Kochba?" Debra turned to Miss Baron for help.

"Debra is right, boys," said Miss Baron.

The boys objected. "But our charade happened before the war. Rabbi Akiba liked peace, and wanted peace," said Richard. The boys all agreed with Richard.

"You are both right," said Miss Baron. "I am glad you remember the story so well. Your turn, girls."

Debra patted David's head. "We have a tough one for you. You'll never guess it in a million years."

When the girls came back Debra stood tall with her arms close to her sides. Judy twisted a long string around and around Debra's body until she looked like a tied-up bundle. Debra looked at the sky and moved her lips as though she were praying. The other girls with branches in their hands stood all around her watching.

Judy said, "Guess!"

The boys stood with puzzled expressions on their faces. This charade was a tough one just as Debra had promised.

Miss Baron looked puzzled, and the mothers shook their heads. They didn't know either.

"Do you give up?" asked Judy. She laughed at the boys.

"Yes!" shouted the boys.

Debra was still a bundle. Judy hadn't tied her mouth so she told them what the charade was all about.

"Well, I'm Rabbi Akiba and I am being put to death because I won't give up my God. But I don't care a bit. I am saying, 'And I shall love the Lord, my God, with all my heart, and with all my soul, and with all my might.' The girls are the Roman soldiers who are doing the cruel deed." Everyone clapped.

"Time to see who is the best archer," Miss Baron said.

Bill pinned the target to the pine tree. Miss Baron and the mothers arranged the children who wanted to shoot the arrows along a straight line, about twenty feet from the target. She announced the rules. The children waited for their turns.

G'dee returned and stood watching.

Judy fitted her arrow into the bow. She stared straight at the bull's-eye. Everyone was quiet. Whiz-z-z-z-z, through the air flew the arrow and landed—in a yellow jonquil. G'dee scampered over to the flower bed, grabbed the arrow in his mouth, and brought it back to Miss Baron.

Richard fitted his arrow into the bow. Looking squarely at the target, he let the arrow go. Whiz-z-z-z-z-z-z, into the air it soared and landed—on the branch of a fir tree. G'dee ran to get the arrow, but he couldn't reach that high. He glared at the unreachable arrow.

David fitted his arrow into the bow. He winked at G'dee. Whir-r-r-r, the arrow whizzed through the blue sky and over the trees. G'dee was a shooting star as he followed the journey of the arrow and disappeared beyond the clearing.

The game continued until everyone had a chance to try his skill.

Debra and Roger and Vicki landed closest to the bull's-eye. Miss Baron gave them a silver m'zuzo.

The children insisted that Bill and Miss Baron try, too. Bill was a good marksman. He hit the bull's-eye square in the middle. Miss Baron aimed her arrow and it landed in the middle of a tulip. The children clapped and shouted.

"You need practice, William Tell," chuckled David.

Miss Baron laughed, "Time to eat!"

The brisk air made everyone hungry. The children ate everything in sight. Miss Baron had no trouble with appetites at all. The children decided to save the Lag Bo-omer eggs. They wanted to take them home to show their parents.

Debra looked around. "Where's G'dee, David?" she asked, just as David was biting into a piece of fudgy chocolate cake with fudgy frosting. David's mouth was full of cake. He swallowed. "Didn't he come back with the arrow, before?"

They ran to Miss Baron, worried about their pet. "He can't be very far away," comforted Miss Baron. "Let's look through the wooded path. He probably stopped to hunt for grasshoppers."

"Not G'dee, Miss Baron. He knew that we had better things to eat," said David. "G'dee's in trouble. I just know it!"

They searched everywhere. They ran into the bird house. No G'dee. They asked the zoo keeper if he had seen a little white goat. The zoo keeper told them that he had noticed a goat with a rainbow beard headed toward the elephant house.

Near the elephant house they spotted a huge crowd of people cheering at the top of their voices. They sounded louder than a baseball game after a home run. The twins ran on wings toward the noise, with Miss Baron bringing up the rear, her face scarlet. They couldn't break through the crowd, but Miss Baron could see over the heads of the crowd because she was tall.

"What do you see?" asked Debra, standing on her tippety toes trying to catch a glimpse.

Miss Baron was speechless. She gulped and gulped again. "Come on, twins we'll have to push our way through. G'dee's in quite a fix. Please let us through," she begged, "that goat belongs to us."

The people separated and made a path for them. A unique scene greeted the twins' eyes. G'dee was perched high on the back of Jumbo, the grey baby elephant. Jumbo was lumbering around the yard shaking his great frayed ears back and forth. G'dee was sitting calmly on his haunches, with his rainbow beard glittering in the sun.

"How did he get in?" asked David.

"How did he get on?" asked Debra.

"How will he get off?" asked Miss Baron, passing her hand over her perspiring forehead.

They saw the elephant keeper come out with a tall ladder. He signaled the elephant to stop, but Jumbo refused. He liked his strange passenger, and he liked the cheers of the crowd. He bowed his head at the applause once, twice, and again. G'dee bowed his pointed head, too. He bowed very carefully. He had his balance to keep. Riding on an elephant required all his skill.

The keeper shouted again at Jumbo to stop, but Jumbo still refused. He tramped around the yard, kicking up the white dust with his clumsy elephant feet.

"G'dee," shouted Debra, "we have to go home!"

"G'dee," shouted David, "make that elephant stop!"

G'dee winked at the twins, and wagged his tail. He waved a paw at them, almost losing his balance. "I like it up here close to the clouds, and I'm not going to get off until I'm good and ready," he bleated.

The crowd roared. Some of the people had cameras and were snapping pictures.

The keeper went back into the elephant house and brought out a load of hay. He followed Jumbo with a heaping pitchfork. Jumbo sniffed and sniffed again. He stopped dead in his tracks. He was conquered. Hay was his favorite food, and he was mighty hungry. With a trumpet of joy he crossed his legs, bent down, and attacked the hay. The keeper leaned the ladder against Jumbo's side, and climbed up, up, up, to the top. G'dee knew that he was licked. He had no place to turn.

Grabbing G'dee's body, the keeper hauled him down to the bottom of the ladder.

"Whose goat is this?" he asked in a gruff voice.

"Over here," called Debra, a little frightened at the anger in the keeper's voice.

"Come around to the front entrance and I'll give him to you," growled the keeper.

When G'dee was in David's arms once more, David asked curiously, "How did G'dee get into the yard?"

"My careless assistant left the small gate to the yard open and your goat walked in as if it were his own house."

"How did G'dee get on Jumbo's back?" asked Debra very curiously.

"Now, how do you think? Jumbo curled his trunk around your goat's body and swung him up on his back," answered the keeper, glaring at G'dee for all the trouble he had caused. "That goat of yours likes danger, I can tell you for sure."

140

"Thank you so much for taking G'dee off Jumbo's back," said Miss Baron, relieved that the adventure had not ended in tragedy.

"Ma-a-a-a-a," bleated G'dee, trying to get out of David's arms to butt the keeper for spoiling his wonderful ride.

They hurried back to the rest of the children. When the twins told the class about G'dee's free ride, the children were disappointed because they had missed the fun.

That night in the *Boston Globe* there was a picture of Jumbo with G'dee on his back. The caption under the picture said, "Painted goat gets a free ride on Jumbo at Franklin Park." There was some more about the twins and their goat.

Debra and David cut out the article and pinned it on the kitchen bulletin board.

G'dee was becoming a famous goat.

G'dee was pleased with himself. He had had the most wonderful Lag Bo-omer of all. Think of it! A ride on an elephant's back! That was exactly how he liked to live. Dangerously!

One
Year
Old

A SUNBEAM DANCED ACROSS G'DEE'S
horn turning it to gold. It glided on to his button nose awak-
ening him early on Shovuos morning. He leaped out of his
swimming pool bed.

"I'm one year old today," he ma-a-a-a-ed to the sunbeam, "and there's going to be a birthday party in my honor
in the back garden."

All was quiet in the house.

Into David's room he dashed. Around and around
David's bed he circled like a rocket with a firecracker tied
to its tail. David opened one sleepy eye and blinked.

"I know. I know. It's your birthday," he laughed, tumbling out of bed with a thump. G'dee cocked his head impatiently, and wiggled his ears like a circus clown. David
kneeled down beside his little pet and hugged him tenderly.

"One pat for your birthday and one pat for good luck,"
he said, as he gave G'dee two whacks exactly where his tail
began.

Next G'dee sprinted into Debra's bedroom, and on to
her bed. He bleated saucily into her ear. Debra snapped
awake.

"I know. I know. It's your birthday," she laughed as she gathered her pet into her arms lovingly. "One pat for your birthday and one pat for good luck," said Debra, giving her goat two spanks on the tip of his turned-up tail.

Into Mr. and Mrs. Mann's bedroom raced G'dee. Around the bed he dashed, around and around, until Daddy threatened him with a slipper.

"Get up! Get up! You lazy people!" bleated G'dee, leaping up at Daddy to get the slipper. "It's my birthday and there's work to be done."

The birthday goat was right. There *was* work to be done, and it had to be finished by nine-thirty that morning. Nobody wanted to be late for the Shovuos services at the temple that day. The boys and girls of the tenth grade in the religious school were going to be confirmed. The twins were excited because this was to be the first Confirmation they had ever attended.

Soon there was a busy hustle about the house. Mother checked the refreshments. Daddy put up a long board on the terrace in back of the house. He balanced the board on two barrels. The guests would be very comfortable eating at this table.

The twins put G'dee through his routine of tricks. G'dee was letter perfect. He would give a star performance at the party.

The twins practiced their surprise entertainment.

At nine-thirty Grandfather and Grandmother arrived in their station wagon. G'dee leaped on Grandfather with his front paws. Grandfather backed away quickly, and brushed his coat.

Debra helped him. "G'dee's extra frisky today because it's his birthday."

Grandfather bent down to kiss Debra's rosy cheek, and give G'dee a birthday pat at the same time. "Shovuos is a popular birthday date, it seems. There's the Ten Commandments given to Moses on Mt. Sinai—and there's King David in the Bible—he was born on Shovuos—and—"

"There's G'dee," finished David with pride.

G'dee crossed his legs and waggled his beard. "Yes, indeedy, I'm in mighty good company today," he bleated to the blue sky.

"Are we ready?" asked Grandfather, climbing into the car to sit beside Grandmother. Daddy and Mother climbed into the car. David and Debra climbed into the car. The door closed and Grandfather quickly stepped on the starter of the car.

"And what about me?" ma-a-a-a-ed G'dee, licking the locked door.

"You'd better shut him up in the garage, David, or he'll follow us to the temple," said Daddy.

David dragged G'dee into the garage and closed the door. The hurt goat stamped his legs at David. "Is this the way to treat a goat on his birthday, especially such an important birthday?" bleated G'dee crossly.

"We'll make it up to him at the party," said Debra, when David came back to the car.

They sped away to the temple.

The happy spirit of Shovuos shone everywhere in the crowded temple. Shiny leaves lay in heaps in the deep window-sills along the side aisles. In the midst of the leaves stood huge vases of peonies. The twins looked with eager eyes at the low fence of branches stretched across the front of the altar. Great pink and red geraniums seemed to grow in the lacy branches. Behind the green fence were the chairs on which the confirmands were to sit.

"The temple looks like a magic garden," said Debra to Grandfather as they sat down near the aisle.

Grandfather squeezed Debra's hand hard. "We make a garden in the temple to show our thanks to God. God makes the beautiful trees and the lovely flowers. This is how we thank Him for His lovingkindness."

At ten o'clock the great organ sounded high in the choir loft. David and Debra sat up eagerly, their eyes bright with interest.

Down the aisles on both sides of the temple to the slow majestic music, they watched thirty-six confirmands march with serious faces. The twins knew that this was an important day in the lives of all the marching boys and girls. On this day of Shovuos they became a grown-up part of the people of Israel. Today they would declare their love for the Jewish religion and promise faithfully to be true to the Ten Commandments given to Moses so long ago on Mt. Sinai.

The girls were lovely in their snowy white robes. Each one carried a graceful sheaf of pink carnations tied with a pink satin bow.

The boys looked handsome in their blue robes.

"There's Sandra. Isn't she beautiful?" said Debra to David just as Sandra passed their row. Sandra's eyes twinkled at the twins for a flashing second, and turned front gazing steadily at the altar.

The boys and girls marched to the altar and sat on the seats behind the green branches. Their shining faces looked out at the congregation, and the services began. From beginning to end the services were conducted by the boys and girls. Each one had something to say in the pageant they had written.

The twins watched the story of Ruth in the Bible come alive before their eyes as the dramatic voices of the confirmands swept them back through the centuries to the land of Moab, and then to the land of Palestine at the time of the barley harvest. Best of all they loved Ruth, the Moabitess, because she was loyal and true to Naomi, her mother-in-law. Debra wanted to cheer when Ruth refused to leave Naomi. During this part of the pageant one of the confirmands sang Ruth's song, "Entreat Me Not to Leave Thee." There was a hushed silence as her golden voice floated out into the audience.

"She sings like an angel," whispered David to Debra.

"Like a golden Shovuos angel," said Debra.

Some of the words were hard for the twins to understand, but David and Debra listened just the same. When Boaz asked Ruth to be his wife, they smiled at each other.

"I'm glad that Boaz and Ruth lived happily ever after," said Debra.

"Ruth really deserved to be the great-great-grandmother of King David," said David with a shake of his head. Daddy nudged them to be quiet. The Torah was being taken out of the Holy Ark.

Robert Golden, another confirmand, stepped up to the marble pulpit. He picked up the carved silver pointer to point to the Hebrew words in the Torah. He looked out at the people.

"Our Jewish religion began when Moses received the Ten Commandments on Mt. Sinai. These laws are the heart and the strength of all our laws of conduct. When the Jews gave the Ten Commandments to the world they made one of the greatest contributions to mankind that the world has ever known." He paused to look at the crowded temple and went on. "We gather in the temple this Shovuos morning to receive the Torah as we do each year. All the civilized peoples of the world base their living on our Ten Commandments."

Robert pointed to the Hebrew words in the Torah with the silver hand. His clear young voice rang out as he read each commandment in Hebrew and translated it into English.

Later the twins watched the rabbi bless the confirmands, two by two, in front of the open Holy Ark. They knew that they, too, would be blessed by the rabbi on the same altar in the same way.

When the service was over, Debra turned to David. "We'll be blessed together because we're twins."

When they came home the twins ran to the garage to get G'dee. The garage door was open, and G'dee was nowhere to be seen. They ran into the backyard.

"G'dee," called David and Debra together in one voice.

"Ma-a-a-a-a," came a faint bleat from one of the barrels on which the long board was balanced.

David and Debra raced over to the barrel. There was their little birthday goat, his head deep in the barrel, his hind legs waving in the air. The twins tugged with all their might. A bedraggled G'dee came out, whimpering painfully. The goat glared at the twins. It was their fault this time for leaving him alone on his birthday.

He lowered his horns and charged at David who was standing in his path. David backed away—back—back—he went, and toppled over into a thorny rose bush.

148

"Ouch!" shrieked David as the thorns pierced his flesh. He leaped into the air like a gazelle.

G'dee smiled his goat smile. "I guess I don't know my own strength."

"Is that the way for a goat to behave who is having a birthday party?" cried David, shaking his fist at G'dee.

To show how sorry he was, he helped Debra take the thorns out of David one by one. Of course, the thorns hopped down G'dee's throat. His tough, rough mouth didn't mind prickly thorns. No, not one bit!

At two o'clock the guests arrived. There were twelve children from the twins' religious school class, and Miss Baron, their teacher. Each one carried a gaily wrapped package for G'dee. Miss Baron carried a heavy red cellophane wrapped basket.

G'dee offered his right paw to each guest. The children heaped their gifts on the grass. The packages looked like a rainbow of flowers against the grass. Some of the gifts had poems attached to them.

"Let's open the gifts now and read the poems," suggested Debra.

"A fine idea," bleated G'dee who was very anxious to know what the pretty packages contained. He had been nosing curiously ever since they were laid on the grass.

Louise was the first. Her gift was a smooth rubber bone. Her poem said:

> Happy birthday, goat, to you,
> Here's a bone for you to chew.

G'dee bowed his head low in thanks and happily chewed on the rubber bone.

Andy opened his gift. In it was a tinkly golden bell and a tinkly silver bell. He tied the bells to G'dee's collar, and read his poem.

> Bells of silver, bells of gold,
> Here's to you, just one year old.

G'dee ran around Andy jingling a "thank you" to him.

Vicki brought a box of red berries. She opened the box and popped a handful into G'dee's mouth. Her poem said:

> Juicy red berries as red as can be,
> Poppity, poppity, into G'dee.

G'dee licked Vicki's hand in grateful thanks.

Elizabeth had a large slipper of rabbit fur. When G'dee saw the slipper he snatched it out of her hand and began to nibble on it furiously. Elizabeth read her poem.

> A slipper is what you prefer,
> So here is one of rabbit fur.

Everyone laughed merrily when G'dee somersaulted his thanks over the slipper and bumped into Elizabeth's legs, knocking her down on the grass.

Miss Baron picked up her basket. Under the cellophane the children could see that she had arranged it just as the farmers in ancient Palestine had arranged theirs when they brought their offerings to the Temple in Jerusalem. On the bottom was a layer of barley, and then a layer of wheat. Spread over the grain were ripe olives and dates and figs. The top and the sides were decorated with shiny leaves. It was Miss Baron's special offering of bikurim, the first-fruits. She threw a fig into G'dee's mouth and read her poem.

> Here's a basket heaped to the brim,
> In Hebrew it's called bikurim.
> To a little goat with a snub-nosed tail,
> To win my heart he'll never fail.

G'dee bowed low to Miss Baron and wagged his tail joyfully. "You know exactly what to bring a goat for Shovuos," he bleated, eating a date from the basket.

Debra unwrapped her present.

> A gift to G'dee
> From David and me.

She held up a blue porcelain dish with a white goat painted inside on the bottom of the plate. On the goat was printed G'DEE. Debra sang her poem looking lovingly at her goat:

> We love the way you cock your head,
> We love the way you eat your bed,
> We're lucky twins you'll all agree,
> To own a playmate like G'dee.

She bent down with the plate to let G'dee look at it. When he saw the white goat he licked it. "I'd rather be a real goat, thank you," he bleated at the painted goat with scorn.

All the children sat in a circle on the grass and sang Shovuos songs. They sang "Dundai" and "Yi-Yi-Yi-Yisroel!" in honor of the birthday of the Ten Commandments.

Mother and Grandmother put the refreshments on the long table on the terrace. There were cheese blintses and honey cakes in honor of the holiday.

"Here I come," announced Grandmother, carrying a huge white frosted birthday cake. The guests' eyes opened

wide. Never had they seen a cake like it. It rose high in the air in three layers, covered with white frosting. On the top was a Torah outlined in blue frosting. Under the Torah was G'DEE in blue frosted letters. In front of G'dee was a tiny blue candle. David lit the candle.

"Happy birthday to you," sang the children. G'dee stared at the cake, licking his lips.

"Blow the candle out, G'dee," said David.

G'dee looked at the bright flame. Edging close to the cake, he huffed and he puffed. The flame flickered for a second but didn't go out.

"Again, G'dee, try harder this time," urged David in an encouraging voice.

G'dee huffed and he puffed—and he puffed and he huffed. The twins held their breaths. The children held their breaths. Would G'dee make it this time? They watched quietly. With a last faint flicker the flame disappeared. The children clapped and cheered. G'dee heaved a sigh of relief. Success lit up his little goat face like an electric bulb.

152

"So-o-o-o-o—what are you waiting for? Get going!" he bleated at the knife in Mother's hand.

Mother cut the cake and served it on paper plates. G'dee gobbled his share in one greedy gulp. He longed for another piece but it was time for his act.

David stood up on the grass like a circus ringmaster.

"My friends, you are about to see some super colossal tricks. Our birthday goat is about to perform."

G'dee was ready, willing and able.

"Bow to the audience, G'dee," said David. G'dee bowed low to the children.

"Cross your front legs." G'dee crossed his right front leg over his left leg, ma-a-a-a-ed at his guests, and winked at the twins.

Debra held up a paper covered hoop.

"Jump through the hoop," commanded David. G'dee turned his back and began to examine Susan's shoe.

David was embarrassed. What was he going to do? A bright idea flashed through his head. Running to the table he snatched a piece of birthday cake.

Racing behind the hoop he held the cake up high. "Here, G'dee, this is for you." He swished the cake around in the air and waited. G'dee soared through the air like a white bird. Through the paper hoop he crashed, landing on the grass with a somersault. Recovering his balance he leaped on David knocking him to the grass. He lapped up the cake before David could give it to him.

Shrieks of merry laughter filled the garden.

Now came the surprise entertainment. Debra was the announcer this time. "Grandfather is going to perform some magic tricks for you, while G'dee and David and Susan, and Jonathan and myself prepare a surprise for you."

The children clapped for Grandfather's tricks, and they clapped for the surprise.

Grandmother and Mother helped the twins. When they were ready, Daddy gave the signal to Grandfather just as he finished pulling a quarter out of Miss Baron's hair.

Around the side of the house came Debra dressed in her Chanuko costume. In her hands she carried a bowl filled with dates and figs and grapes. Following her came G'dee. On each horn was a wreath of leaves, and around his neck was a string of sunny yellow jonquils. Then came David blow-

ing a wild tune on his horn. He wore a long blue striped robe tied with a blue rope. Susan and Jonathan walked together behind David. Susan carried two loaves of bread, and Jonathan had two long golden sheaves of wheat in his arms. They formed a circle around G'dee, and danced gaily while David tooted his horn until he was red in the face.

Miss Baron was delighted with the clever act.

Debra giggled at the wondering children. "Guess where we're going?" she asked.

The children couldn't guess at all. They scratched their heads.

"Give up?" asked Debra, flashing a dimple at her guests.

G'dee ate a jonquil while he was waiting.

"*We give up!*" shouted the children.

Debra explained the act with a poem.

> Pilgrims all
> Hear the call,
> To Jerusalem we go.
> Best of fruit
> Best of grain
> To the Lord our gifts bestow.
>
> Flowers bright
> Deck the horns
> Of the ox who leads the way.
> Sound the flute,
> Sweet the tune
> On this happy Shovuos day.
>
> Marching feet
> Down the road
> To the Lord our praises sing.
> Loaves of bread,
> Sheaves of wheat
> To the Temple gaily bring.
>
> Share the crops,
> Offer thanks
> To the Lord for loving care.
> Pilgrims we,
> Marching free,
> In our hearts a gladsome prayer.

Debra looked down at G'dee with a fond smile. G'dee winked at her. "Oh, ho, so I'm an ox now," he bleated.

"We're the ancient Pilgrims of Palestine. We're on our way to Jerusalem, and the time is Shovuos. We are bringing the first-fruits of the harvest from our gardens to the Temple as an offering of thanks to God for His loving care."

G'dee nibbled another jonquil from the string around his neck. He shook a leaf off the wreath on his horn.

Miss Baron ran over to get her bikurim basket. She placed it on the grass in front of Debra. "This belongs in the act, too," she said.

G'dee looked at her, and he ran over to the stand beside the basket. "Be careful how you handle my best present," he bleated at Miss Baron.

Daddy dragged a ladder to a spot on the grass. Grandfather dragged another ladder to a place opposite the first ladder. Across the tops of the ladders they put a long board about two feet wide.

G'dee looked at the ladders. Now he was really going to have fun! He needed no urging this time. Up one ladder he clambered. Across the board he tripped, looking out nonchalantly at his audience, very much at home on his new trapeze. Down the other ladder he climbed, his beard jutting out like a waving flag. The children cheered. G'dee didn't pause for a second except for a graceful bow to the children.

Up and across and down he frisked like an acrobat, not one bit afraid of his death-defying act. Poof! and another poof! This was easy—and fun to boot!

The children watched, their mouths watering. Oh, how they longed to be doing what G'dee was doing!

"I wish that I could try it," said Wendy, wistfully, to Debra.

No sooner said than done. Daddy stationed himself at one ladder. Grandfather stationed himself at the other ladder, and Miss Baron took care of the middle. The children played "Follow the Leader." G'dee was the leader.

Suddenly the air was pierced by a loud voice.

"Does G'dee Mann live here?—I rang the bell but there was no answer. When I heard all the laughing out in the back I came in." A tall man stood on the grass, dressed in a delivery man's uniform.

The twins ran over to the man.

"G'dee Mann is our little goat and we're having a birthday party for him," giggled Debra, looking up at the man.

"G'dee Mann is a goat!" exclaimed the man in surprise.

"Well—I never—there's a crate for him from the State of Israel."

The driver disappeared around the front of the house and came back, lugging a crate with holes on the top. He set it down on the terrace, gave Daddy a paper to sign, and walked away, scratching his head and muttering to himself.

Everyone gathered around. What could it be?

G'dee tried to climb up the sides but David held him back. A sharp bleat ripped the air.

An answering bleat came from G'dee who tried desperately to get away from David's clutches.

Daddy pried off the lid. In the box was a little white goat, the spitting image of G'dee.

Daddy gently lifted the goat out and set it on the grass. Like a homing pigeon the new visitor headed straight for G'dee. Their horns tapped hello to each other. Their tongues licked each other's faces.

Friendship gleamed in their eyes. Daddy looked at Mother. Grandfather looked at Grandmother. Miss Baron looked at all of them.

Nobody said a word.

Daddy found a note inside the crate. He read it aloud to everyone.

> *Dear G'dee:*
>
> I know that you are very happy with David and Debra. They have told me how much they love you. Still and all you must be lonely when they go off to school. So, for your birthday, on this happy Shovuos day, I am sending you a new playmate with whom to play when the twins are busy. Her name is G'deeda. I hope you will welcome her. Happy Birthday!
>
> With love,
> UNCLE JOSEPH

David smiled at Debra, and Debra smiled at David.

"Look," said David, "G'dee and G'deeda are friends already."

And indeed they were. They were chasing each other through the flower beds, tickling their noses in the fragrant blossoms.

Daddy looked at Mother and Mother looked at the trampled flower beds. She sighed. "Most families have a dog and a cat. So—why can't we have two goats?"

The twins flew into her arms, hugging her until she shouted for help.

Daddy borrowed another swimming pool and filled it with sweet grass.

Everyone slept soundly that night. Mother dreamed about millions of goats—dashing around her living-room. Daddy dreamed about millions of goats—tearing up his velvety smooth lawns. Debra dreamed about millions of goats—running around Temple Israel. David dreamed about millions of goats—doing trapeze tricks on the roof of the ranch house.

But in their twin swimming pools G'dee and G'deeda were having a long conversation. G'dee was doing all the talking and G'deeda was doing all the listening. Her two ears were pointed upward in excitement.

"You'll love the jolly Mann family," bleated G'dee. "They'll take you into their hearts just as they have taken me into their hearts. They'll share their fun with you just as they have shared their fun with me. And oh, G'deeda, how you'll love celebrating all the Jewish holidays with David and Debra."

G'deeda wagged her tail with a bleat of contentment.

"But best of all—yes, best of all—will be the warm feeling you have being a Jewish goat." G'dee wagged his snubnosed tail with happiness. "Yes, G'deeda, it is the most wonderful adventure in the world to be a Jewish goat."

GLOSSARY

afikomon	the special name for the dessert matso.
arbo-o	four
Atzai Zaisim Omdim	Hebrew for "Olive Trees Are Standing," name of a song.
Bar Kochba	Hebrew for "Son of a Star," name of the Jewish leader who fought against the Romans about 135 C.E.
bikurim	first-fruits
blintses	cheese rolls
b'rayshis	Hebrew for "in the beginning," the first word of the Torah.
Chad Gadyo	Aramaic for "One Kid," the Passover song describing his adventures.
challoh	Special bread for Shabos and holidays, generally with a twisted top.
Chamisho Osor Bi-Sh'vot	Hebrew for 15th day of the month Sh'vot; the Jewish New Year of the trees or Arbor Day.
chamisho	five
Chanuko	Festival of Dedication, celebrating the victory of the Maccabees in their fight for religious freedom.
charoses	mixture of apples, nuts, cinnamon, and wine.
chomets	anything leavened, and, as such, not to be eaten during Passover.
dreidel	top with four sides, used on Chanuko.
echod	one
esrog	the citron, a fruit of the land of Israel that looks like a lemon.

160

g'dee	goat
gragger	noisemaker
haggadah	literally "the telling"; the name given to the book which tells the story of Passover and gives the rituals for the Seder.
hakofos	Hebrew for circling around, the ceremony of carrying the Torahs around the synagogue on Simchas Torah.
homontaschen	three-cornered cakes filled with poppy seeds.
hora	favorite dance in the State of Israel.
Keren Ami	Hebrew for "Fund of My People," name often used for religious school charity collections.
Kiddush	prayer over the wine for Shabos and the festivals.
Kohanim	the Hebrew word for "priests."
Kol Nidrei	Hebrew for "all vows"; the name of the serious prayer with which the Yom Kippur evening services proper begin.
Lag Bo-omer	33rd day of the counting of the omer.
latkes	potato pancakes
Levites	the assistant priests who served along with them.
lulov	a palm sheaf together with twigs of willow and myrtle make up the Sukos symbol we call the lulov.
matso	unleavened bread
megillah	Hebrew for "Scroll," name given to the book of Esther.
menorah	many-branched candleholder.
Meron	place in Israel where Rabbi Simeon ben Yochai lived.
moror	bitter tasting plants
nes godol hoyo shom	sentence made of letters on the sides of the dreidel "N-G-H-SH," meaning "a great miracle happened there."

omer	a Hebrew measuring term, like "bushel," used as the name of the period after Passover when 50 days are counted to get to Shovuos.
Pesach	Hebrew name for "Passover," the Spring holiday celebrating the freeing of the Jews from Egyptian slavery.
Purim	Hebrew for "Lots," the holiday celebrating the escape of the Jews of Persia from Haman through the courage of Esther and Mordecai.
Rabbi Akiba	famous rabbi and teacher of the Torah about 135 C.E.
Rabbi Simeon ben Yochai	student of Akiba's, famous rabbi and teacher of the Torah.
Rosh Ha-shono	Hebrew for "head of the year," meaning the beginning of the year and thus the name for the festival of the New Year.
Seder	Hebrew for "order"; name given to rituals at the dinner table the first night of Passover which follow a set "order."
Shabos	Hebrew for "stopping, rest"; generally, the name given to the seventh day, "The Sabbath."
Shalach Monos	Hebrew for "sending of gifts"; name of the Purim custom.
Shalom	Hebrew for "peace," but also hello, good-bye.
shamos	Hebrew for "servant"; here the servant candle who lights the other candles on the menorah.
sh'losho	three
sh'nayim	two
shofor	horn taken from a ram and used to sound calls during the High Holy Days.

Sholom Aleichem	Hebrew for "welcome," traditional Shabos song used to welcome the day.
Shovuos	Hebrew for "weeks"; name of the holiday celebrating the giving of the Torah, which comes 7 weeks and a day after Passover.
sh'vorim	one of the traditional shofor calls, a low note followed by a high one, three times, quickly.
Simchas Torah	Hebrew for "Rejoicing of the Law"; name of the last day of Sukos.
suko	booth
Sukos	Feast of Booths
t'kio	one of the traditional shofor calls, a low note followed by a high one.
t'ruo	one of the traditional shofor calls, one note quickly stopped several times followed by a higher note.
Tu Bi-Sh'vot	"Tu" is the shortened form of writing 15 in Hebrew; short for chamisho osor.
Yom Kippur	the Day of Atonement, the most serious single day of the Jewish calendar, spent seeking forgiveness from God for our sins.
Z'miros	joyous Sabbath songs traditionally sung at the table.

UNION GRADED SERIES

EDITED BY

EMANUEL GAMORAN, PH.D., *Director of Education*
Union of American Hebrew Congregations